we were one once

book 1

Books by Willow Madison

True Nature

True Beginnings

True Choices

True Control 4.1

True Control 4.2

we were one once 2

Existential Angst

the SAYER

we were one once

book 1

Willow Madison

Madison, Willow

we were one once (One, Book One)

Front Cover Design by David Colon (www.colonfilm.com); Back Cover Design by XIX (www.thenineteen.net)

Edit by Q (www.editingbyq.com)

This is a work of fiction. Names, characters, places and incidents are either the product of the author's imagination or are used fictitiously, and any resemblance to actual persons, living or dead, business establishments, events or locales is entirely coincidental.

This book is intended for adults only. Spanking and other sexual activities represented in this book are fantasies only, intended for adults. Nothing in the book should be interpreted as advocating any non-consensual spanking activity or the spanking of minors.

www.willowmadisonbooks.com

ISBN-13: 978-0-9963191-1-9
ISBN-10: 0-9963191-1-5

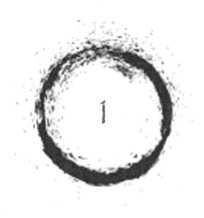

San Francisco: Simon Lamb

Watching. It's the first thrill I get. I like this part—the beginning, watching. Sometimes it's from afar, but usually I'm up close. I try to get as close as I can. I like to smell. To hear. For me, it's all about the senses. I'm a product of my environment, and I need to have constant stimulation. I chuckle to myself with this thought.

I touched this one once. In a store, I reached for the same can of soup on purpose. Her hand sprang away like I'd grabbed *it* instead.

That was a good day, the day I first laid eyes on her. She dropped the can. I thought it landed on her foot, but it only rolled away. She didn't even look at it or me, just walked away. She left her cart and walked away.

I like this one. She's special. They're all special to me; but this one, she's different. And it's not just because she's plain. Everything about her is plain. Kinky brown hair that hasn't seen a brush in a long time hides large brown eyes that only dart around occasionally before they shoot down to the ground again. No makeup, and she's so tiny, not even taking up half the seat she's in. This one's not my usual object of sexual desire and definitely not what anyone would call an ideal candidate for sex slave of the year.

I chuckle again but manage to cover this with a cough. The crazy Chinese bitch next to me keeps eyeballing me. I glare at her, and she finally gets up from her window seat just as the bus starts to enter the tunnel that bisects the streets lined with downtown storefronts from those fringed with pallets of food in Chinatown.

I glance back at my girl. Plain as she is, there's something about her. Something I saw right away. Something I smelled right away. This one smells like heaven. When she talks, her voice is almost musical, not lyrical but like a tempo beat that she stops and starts at the oddest points. It's a rhythm all her own. And I like that she doesn't talk much. It's a relief from all the fucking chatty bitches in the world, all on their phones non-stop with their non-stop chatter. It drives me fucking nuts.

I stand as the bus rocks to a stop and shove past a couple of suits and a hot fuck in leggings standing in the aisle. My height and build give me an advantage over the throng of passengers trying to get on or off. I make my way onto the street easily, past all of their pink plastic bags stuffed with bok choy, frogs, and an assortment of nasty smelling dried foods.

I don't turn around and say bye to my girl. This isn't goodbye; she'll get off at the next stop. She hasn't looked up anyway, not for the last few blocks.

I didn't try to get close to her this time, just kept watching her from three seats away. I grin knowing that our time for getting real close is fast approaching now.

What the fuck?!

Where is she going?

Alarm bells go off in my head and chest. I don't like this. I don't like anything besides the routine. I know her pattern by now. She should've gotten off the bus at the next stop.

I always get off two blocks before her. Then she gets off. She walks the two blocks uphill to her scummy little apartment above the tea store. I walk by her as she goes up the three steps.

That is our routine, not her fucking staying on the bus!

So why is she fucking with me today and not getting off now?

I jog to catch up with her at the next stop but have to slow myself to a walk when I get close. A tall, strongly built, blond man in Chinatown stands out. It's been her one flaw, living here. I've not been able to hang out around her apartment as quietly as I'd like.

She's still on the bus. I stop. I turn around.

I have discipline. I can wait for her to come back. Whatever she's up to now, it won't matter soon enough.

I look at my watch. It's 5:56 p.m. She hasn't been out later than 7:49 p.m. before. I won't have to wait long. She's a hermit.

I head towards the Szechuan restaurant located diagonally across from her steps. I can keep an eye out for her through the window, eat some noodles, and wait.

I smile at the sweet little hostess as she shows me to a table. She's not *my* type, but I know a buyer who'd pay to play with her. And she smells like cinnamon.

I don't make it obvious that I'm watching the building across the street. I push my body against the cold window but keep my face out of the fluorescent lighting and pull the brim of my cap down more.

This one's never looked up at me, never acknowledged that she's seen me. I don't want to take any chances though, not this close.

For now, I'll stay in the shadows. Watching.

This one will be mine soon enough. Won't be long now, Grace. I hide a grin, trying to imagine what surprise will look like on her normally blank face.

2

Seattle: Miles Vanderson

Facing away from my office door, I take a moment to center my thoughts. From my lofty vantage point, the snaking boardwalk lights of Bell Harbor are starting to brighten against the darkening sky. The cacophony of clinking from sailboat riggings is barely audible through glass thickened to withstand the harsh Northwestern weather. I take a deep, calming breath in and wish for the salt in my lungs. If only these windows could open.

With a measure of control that I don't truly feel, I turn in time to see my door opening. "Spencer, glad you could check in before I have to take off tonight. You have news about Gillian?" I direct the man to sit on a sofa, choosing the chair to his right for myself.

Spencer puts his bag on the coffee table and pulls out a large laptop, old-school to a fault. I wave off my assistant, indicating that the door should be closed behind her. She leaves in silence, quickly.

My irritation has been evident all day. Spencer is only the latest in a long line of investigators I've hired over the past three years to search for Gillian. Each one has disappointed me. In this age of information and technology, you would think finding one small girl would be easy! With my vast fortune, you would think it would be even easier.

Our family has always garnered the attention of the press, but never more so than when my stepsister went missing three years ago. Every detective for hire in the country knew the names Gillian Starck and Miles Vanderson then. In the beginning, they resembled salmon forcing their way up hatchery ladders, churning up every square inch of Seattle in an attempt to look busy and useful. They all wanted a chance at the large reward I offered.

I ended up hiring the agency with the best track record, both for finding missing women and for keeping quiet about any details. I paid a premium price to keep my family's name out of any potentially sordid stories. And still, every detective has failed to provide me with any useful information, leaving me with only a cold trail.

"Mr. Vanderson, I'm afraid I don't really have much to report." Spencer responds to my arched brows, "*Yet*, Sir. I'm following a few new leads though. Let me show you…"

"I fired your former boss, Spencer, because his agency failed to produce any concrete news on Gillian. He exhausted all of my patience." I sit forward to look at his computer but keep my fingers steepled in front of me, a copy of a look my father employed often; he used it to intimidate and exude calm, controlled anger. I think I do a better job with it.

"Of course, Sir." He pulls up copies of documents, old emails, stubs from ATMs, and transcripts from interviews. "But I think I may have found where Miss Starck went *after* she left Seattle."

I lower my chin onto my fingers and rest my eyes on a far wall to conceal the excitement this news generates in me. "Go on." My voice only betrays my longing by a slight ratchet in its depth.

San Francisco: Simon Lamb

Another look at my watch, it's 9:03 p.m. Grace still isn't here. My hands are sledgehammers at the ends of my corded arms.

I have to loosen up. I'm in public. The dragon-embraced streetlights only provide a sickening glow, but it's enough for anyone to see that I don't belong in this quiet neighborhood now.

I had to leave the restaurant; I couldn't sit there any longer and go unnoticed. I smell like Dim Sum. This whole fucking block smells like it. I won't leave until she's home, but I can't stay on the street. I wish I'd driven over here.

I make a decision. It's early, but I'm ready for her. I'll have to get my car and come back. But tonight, Grace, you're mine.

I smile, relaxing now that I have a plan.

I take the three steps up Grace's shitty building with the smell of the closed tea shop filling my nose. I already have a key. This is the easiest part. Money buys a way in every time. Doors, locks, alarms—they never matter to me.

I'm in and out, never noticed, never stopped.

Her apartment is just as I remember it. Three weeks ago I was in here, checking her out. There's no roommate and no pictures. It's just a furnished SRO with nothing personal added except a few childish drawings on the table and in the trash.

I wondered if she had a kid at first, but I never saw one. No one comes here. No other kid stuff lying around either— so no kid, so not off limits.

I decided that it must be a neighbor's kid. I've seen a few of them hanging around her by the bus stop in the mornings. It's the only time she smiles. It's a tentative, secretive smile even then, hidden behind her dark hair or under her hand. Grace's eyes always remain unreadable, even with that tiny smile.

Walking around her apartment, I can see it's the same as when I was here before. Her underwear is the four-pack variety, no frills. No thrills for me imagining her in them either, but they smell nice. Bleached and neatly folded, they're nondescript just like all her other clothes.

Grace is a clean girl. She smells like bleach and soap, never perfume, never makeup. It's my idea of heaven. This place smells old and musty, yet there's still a hint of her here.

Her clothes are like her too—plain, colorless, brown or black, oversized. She layers so many pieces together she looks like a homeless chick afraid to leave anything behind. She's small, like a child, but I don't even know what her body looks like under all that. I'll find out soon enough though. A grin spreads my face wider.

I satisfy myself that everything is exactly the same, neat and tidy. Dishes are left out to dry next to the small sink. Fridge has milk, OJ, lunchmeat and bread in it. She keeps her sugary cereal in here too. Smart. This building probably has rats.

I lie down on her small bed to wait for her. The springs creak and roll in protest of my greater weight. I idly wonder if they'll break when we're on it together.

Seattle: Miles Vanderson

Stuck in traffic, tail lights expand with endless tendrils of rain along the windshield. My driver leans into the steering wheel to focus more intently on the rush hour jam of vehicles. The constant drum of raindrops on the roof is almost soothing, and I'm grateful for the time to think about what Spencer was able to uncover.

It's been three years since I've seen Gillian, and that means three long years of searching for her. I've given a lot of thought to her whereabouts, what she could have been doing all this time, and why she ran.

I'd rather be heading home, thinking about her as usual. It's about the time I'd normally be having a stiff drink and getting a blowjob at the end of a long day, but business must come first. Even four years after his death, I can't go against the puritan work ethic my father instilled in me. Martin Vanderson ran a tight ship, and no one, certainly not his only son, was allowed to slack off for any reason. I'm still controlled by his drive to achieve. It's my drive now.

Four years ago, the old bastion died on his way to a meeting about acquiring a nagging competitor. It was on this very road. I think of this whenever I head to Sea-Tac airport; but now, with this news of Gillian, I'm thinking back to that night in more detail.

Martin Vanderson, Chairman and CEO of Vanderson Industries, was dead before the ambulance arrived on scene. A heart attack did him in before his injuries. Gillian's mother, Anya, died that night too, though not right away. Gillian and I waited through her surgery, waited through her recovery. We acted appropriately relieved when she woke up. I held Gillian, supported her through it all.

To all observers, we were the portrait of the devoted family torn asunder by the whims of fate. But I knew it was karma. It was karma driving the bus that skidded on the bridge and slammed into the limo carrying our parents. I knew it when my father died. I knew it when her mother died later that night.

"Complications," the doctor said, "infection, internal bleeding, swelling." Karma.

I remember Gillian's dark eyes never divulged the fear I knew she really felt. She was afraid of her mother waking up. I know she was silently praying that she'd die without ever opening her soulless eyes again, that she'd never utter another vile word to her. It was my prayer too, for her and for me, for us.

Gillian's thin legs trembled when the doctors said Anya had regained consciousness. I had to pull her off the waiting room's worn chair and shake her out of her blank stare. I had to force her to act properly, make her walk towards the recovery room with me.

I kept Gillian close to me and held her up; I was a constant physical reminder to stay calm and controlled. She showed no fear. Her wide-open eyes just took everything in like she always did.

Anya did wake up but only briefly. It was only long enough to suffer a little with the pain before drifting off into never never hell where she belonged. Gillian kept the same vacant look upon hearing the news and the entire drive home. She never showed her relief through the wakes, the funerals, or while listening to the will. She stayed frozen long after their deaths. She didn't even show me her true feelings.

Our lives may have changed that night, but everything stayed the same with one main difference. As the sole link to any form of family and with a small financial nudge, at the young age of 22, I was authorized to become the guardian of my 16 year old stepsister fairly quickly. Gillian was allowed to stay in what is now my home, and I was able to continue providing for her well-being as I committed to learning the ropes of Vanderson Industries. I was able to keep Gillian safe and with me. My ultimate plan worked, and I was closer than ever to seeing it to completion.

I lost my father that night, but I gained access to a world of control and power that would have taken me years to gain under his watchful glare. Martin Vanderson never would've let me have the reins so early. I would have withered waiting for my chance to have what I wanted. If given the choice, the old man would've lived forever, I'm sure.

With him in the way, I never would've had what I really wanted, Gillian free from her Mother. He was never around enough to see what went on. He married Anya because she was young enough to give him more children. Anya Starck was only 31 when she became Mrs. Martin Vanderson, the beautiful vessel of his future child that she carried down the courthouse aisle. He craved Anya because her shining example of her own perfection, Gillian, was exactly what he wanted to reproduce. And even though Anya lost that promised future after only three weeks of marriage, he believed he'd have his chance for more children with her.

After two years of marriage, I knew the reason she failed to make due on her end. Still, my father kept Anya close, forcing her to accompany him on longer business trips so he'd have access to her. Despite his efforts, she failed to provide him with more heirs. He was a waning old man, holding out hope. My own mother was his third wife, and I was his sole child from that failed union. Anya didn't stand a chance.

His obsession with having more heirs was Gillian's salvation, though, and mine. Her mother was forced to be in that limo with my father, accompanying him to meetings on the east coast. They died that night so Gillian and I could live on. In peace. That's what I thought as I left the hospital with my stepsister pressed to my side that night.

It's what I still think, driving down this same road across the same bridges. Peaceful, content, fulfilled, happy: these are words I've not known for three long years because Gillian ran away. She left after only one year under my roof. She ran from the safety of being with me into the unknown, and I've been searching for her ever since.

Spencer has a lead though. All my money, all my influence, and I've only ever been able to trace her to the nearest city, Seattle. There she drained a few bank accounts, an impressive sum. The bank manager still won't admit what she must have done to convince him to withdraw those amounts. She had the access codes, the passwords, and the signatures; but she got him to transfer and withdraw the money without alerting anyone, without alerting me. He also helped to make it all untraceable, or nearly.

I've never found any information on what happened to Gillian after she left Seattle. She ran with enough money to hide for a good length of time if she was smart, and Gillian's smart.

After all these years, though, Spencer has a lead. It's a miniscule speck of information that follows her from Seattle to San Francisco, but it's something. It's more than I've had in a long time. It's hope.

I turn to the car window and see my tired reflection in the dark storm. I look older than my 26 years. It's the suit. It's that and the small lines around my dark eyes, the determined set to my mouth and strong jawline, the dark hair kept so short it fades into the darkness of my reflection. I know I have the look of a man of power beyond his years. I've had women tell me it's sexy, that I'm handsome with how powerful I look. I have the Vanderson build. I'm masculine and athletic, not hulking, not bulky, but lithe and muscular. Looking down at my hands holding firm to my knees, I see the strength. I'll need all of it to get through the next few weeks. It'll help me to hold on to that hope.

"Traffic should get moving here soon, Mr. Vanderson." I only nod at my driver's interruption to my thoughts.

San Francisco: Simon Lamb

The buzz from the lit sign right outside her window stops. I look at my watch in the weak light; it's 5:37 a.m.

Hmm. Grace didn't come back. I lift myself from her bed to sit with my shoes on the stained tile floor. Hmm. She starts work at 9:00 a.m. I decide to wait here for a few more hours.

It's dangerous to do this in the morning, but I've done it before. I prefer the cover of night, but for Grace, I'll make an exception.

And I'll make her pay for it. I smile, getting up to help myself to a bowl of cereal.

Parking on a hill, I grab my cap again from the passenger seat. I hate this part of the city almost as much as I hate Chinatown. My body revolts against the press of people. Their smells all mingle.

My anger from this morning is increasing again with each step down the street. Grace never showed.

At least in this area, I don't stand out. I do, but it's because these fuckers think I'm one of them. Or they hope I am. Two twinks smile at me as I pass under the large rainbow flag. Their scrawny shoulders and high voices resemble teenage boys, but they're in their twenties. I growl at them and probably just made their cocks stiff.

I slow down as I near the storefront around the corner. It's a small shop, full of shit twinks would love—tiny t-shirts, porn, collars and leashes, a few hardcore bondage pieces. There's always a gagging display of incense too.

I was surprised to see that this is where she works, surprised for a lot of reasons. She's shy for one. I've not heard Grace speak to a stranger unless it's in this shop, and then it's only to ask and answer as part of her job. She barely makes eye contact. Maybe she's a wanna-be mufflicker? No, I don't think so. She doesn't act any differently around other chicks. Everybody's off limits with Grace.

I liked that from the beginning. I don't think she's a virgin. That'd be too much to hope. I'm not dumb enough to believe that shit in this day. She's young, maybe 20, but I don't buy that she's that innocent. She's never been anything but shy and quiet in the four weeks I've watched her though. No men. No women. No one.

So, the fact that she works around the sex shit was surprising enough, but then there's the astrology crap too. She helps out with the front sometimes, but mostly she runs a table in the back doing astrological charting. She'll tell your past, present, or future using a computer. She's popular and apparently accurate according to the idiots that eat that shit up.

As I open the door, I can hear a guy complaining that he can't get his reading for this weekend. I have to take a deep breath against the assault of incense burning.

"Well, *where* is she? Will she be in by lunch?" The guy looks conventional enough; he's clean cut, wearing a suit and tie. I've seen him in here on weekends with bareass leather chaps and a collar. Grace puts paper towels down for him, but she never makes a face or even acts like it's different. She treats everyone the same—cold and distant.

No one gets past the blank looks and unemotional eyes of my girl.

I liked that from the beginning too. It's what drew me to her. I want to see those dark eyes open wide with emotion, specifically from pain and fear.

"Sorry, Ed. She's never late. I don't even have a phone number for Grace to contact her. Do you want me to call you as soon as she comes in? I'm sure she can have a reading ready for you pretty quickly…" The owner's a white-haired hippy type. He would've been a twink back in his day, but now he settles for being one of the proud survivors of the '80's. He and his partner act fatherly with Grace, but she never acts like she notices. They get the same cold treatment as everybody else.

Shit. She's not here either.

I don't make eye contact, just turn back around and walk out the door.

My anger is percolating again. I'm going to have to decide. Stay around here in this cesspool of too many people, all a little too interested in a guy like me, or go back to her place.

I decide her place is the safest bet.

Fog is just starting to recede over the hill behind the flag as I head back up to my car.

Grace never shows. I lost her.

San Francisco: Simon Lamb

"Mr. Lamb?" I turn around and see a beautiful pair of tits, topped off with a set of puffed up lips and cheekbones and dyed bleached blonde hair. There's a lingering of strong perfume in the air. She tries to smile at me, showing off her perfect teeth. The one I broke has been fixed to match the others nicely.

"Luanne. You look different." She's uncomfortable. Her face has a slight sheen over all the makeup. I can smell her subtle change too. Fear gives an acidic wash over her clinging floral perfume. The panels of her long black dress shake against the floor, and she holds a glass of champagne with too tight a grip.

She lowers her head. "My Master is waiting." Luanne turns, and I watch her walk a little. I wait for her to turn around.

The lobby isn't crowded. Most of the people are in the main ballroom by now, but Luanne still attracts stares from hungry men. Troy, her Master, likes to keep his toys in shape. He also prefers a Barbie-type and makes over any girl that doesn't fit this image right away. Luanne was already close, but I can see the implants and fillers she's gotten since I finished her training. She's nearing the end of her time as one of Troy's favorites. He keeps his girls though, never brokers them again anyway.

I beckon her with my index finger to come back to where I stand. Her face changes. The small amount of fear from a moment ago is replaced by a full dose. It's been two years, but she hasn't forgotten what I did to her, what I'm capable of doing to her still. She wears a mask of seduction, though, as she returns to face me.

"Tell Troy to come himself. *By* himself." As she moves to turn again, I grab her wrist with hardly any pressure. It's like a hot poker to her skin. She jerks and freezes. Her mask is back in place before she looks up at me though. I do good work. "Forget something?"

One tear moves from the inside of her left eye down her cheek. She shakes her head slightly before lowering it, deeper this time, and her voice shakes. "May I go, Sir?"

"Yes, Luanne." But I don't let her hand go. I bring it up to my lips and give it a soft kiss, barely touching her. She's not mine anymore, but I like the saltiness of her skin. I lick my lips as she quickly walks away, wiping her face and smoothing her dress. Her head stays down until she reaches the doors to the ballroom.

I head into the noise of the ballroom too while waiting for Troy. The room is busy. There's round tables for dining, a large dance floor in the front with a band, side tables for wine tastings, and bars everywhere. It's not my sort of thing. I prefer a quiet spot for my deals.

I stay on the edge away from people as much as possible, grabbing a glass of champagne from a passing waiter. I feel a hand on my shoulder, slapping hard. I turn slowly to my left to look down on Troy. Luanne is standing several feet away with one of his men; her chin is lowered almost to her chest.

"Simon! It's always good to see you, my friend. It's like Christmas when you're around!" Troy is loud. Stupid. I move my champagne glass from my left hand to my right. I grab his neck and squeeze with my free hand.

"Ya wanna be discreet, Troy?" I apply just a bit more pressure. "My business requires discretion, as you know…so if you can't be…tell me, *friend*, and we'll end our dealings now." I want to spit his powder smell out of my mouth.

I know I can crush his windpipe, even with my weaker hand. He has one moment to answer correctly before he's unable to do so. I'll leave his ass choking and coughing right here. And I'll up my fee.

"Yes…discre…" I let go of his throat and push him against the empty bar we're near. He chokes and holds his throat but manages to look like he's adjusting his tie instead. I grin.

"Do you want your product?"

He looks around nervously. "You brought her here?"

I nod. "In the car around the corner." I smile a little more, showing a little teeth this time. "The valet is keeping an eye on her."

Troy laughs. "Perfect." He turns to the man standing by Luanne and snaps his fingers. He whispers in his ear but turns to me with a question. "Still driving the same?" I grin in answer. "Go fetch and wait in my car with my new toy," he finishes commanding his bodyguard.

When the man leaves, Troy reaches in his pocket for his phone. He busily pushes in a few codes, swipes a few screens, then puts his phone away with a smug smile. My own phone vibrates silently in my pocket. With the transaction complete, I nod and turn to leave.

"You're not staying for the wine auction, Simon? My family has a special vintage I think you'd appreciate…"

I turn back and grin again, showing a little of the hardness I'm known for. Troy's face drops, and a wary pinch takes over his features. "Sure, I always like to support a good charity." I head to the nearest bar. Troy leads Luanne back to his table without another glance at me.

The point to socializing like this is lost on me. Dressing up, throwing money around to act like a big shot—I don't get it. I have money. I was born with it. Generations of my family haven't had to work for anything. I can have whatever I want, whatever money will buy. And believe me, that's everything.

It's why I do the work I do; I like to challenge myself. I smile into my glass of wine. That's a lie. I do it because I fucking enjoy it.

Looking around here at all these women dressed up, led around by pencil pricked assholes, I know they think they own the world if they're beautiful, young, and even a little intelligent. They think they're secure, tottering around on heels and gliding overly inflated lips across teeth overly whitened.

My first challenge was one of these women. She was a daughter to my grandfather's friend and six years older than me, give or take. I was a horny sixteen year old she thought to teach. I taught her to cry for me. I left my scars on her, inside and out. I owned her for the rest of her miserable little life. She killed herself before her wedding night. I guess she didn't think her father's choice of mate would appreciate seeing my initials carved into her skin.

I've learned since then to take better care of my toys, to not leave any lasting marks. New owners are touchy on this point. They'll pay top price for pristine product, or nearly pristine.

And I've learned to not shit where I eat too. I don't mess with the women in my own circle anymore. They don't make for good product anyway—too needy, too spoiled, no fun, no challenge.

I have other limitations. No homeless, no one under eighteen, no mothers—it's a short list, but I've stuck with it. The homeless and underage are too weak, too easy. The mother thing…well, whatever.

I move a little more into the room. I smile at those I recognize, those that recognize me. There are only a few clients here tonight. Only Troy brings his toys out, but he's never been married. He can parade whatever he likes without taking a hit to his reputation. He knows he still has to be inconspicuous though. You'd have to look closely to see that Luanne isn't the same as the other women here.

My clients have to meet strict criteria too. Besides proving they're able to be discreet, they have to be known to me already or introduced to me by someone that is. They have to be very specific on likes and dislikes. I won't hand my product off to a limp dick who can't appreciate my work. A firm hand is needed with my girls long after I've trained them to accept it as their lot in life. Clients also have to be willing to accept my golden rule—absolutely no interference in my selection or training process.

In return, they get a fully submissive, pliant, and trained to their tastes product to own and use. There are no refunds, no returns, and no negotiations. I don't want or need to know what happens after payment, but I have no doubt if there were a review site for this sort of shit, I'd have five stars.

I head to a table near the edge of the dance floor. "Peter, Craig, good to see you guys." I shake hands with two of the men at the table and nod to their dates.

"What's Batman doing out of his cave tonight?" Craig stands to be next to me.

"Ha! Joke never gets old." I set my glass of wine down on their table and see how Peter's fiancée watches me. I banged her two years ago, right after she met him. She's been trying to get my attention again ever since. She was okay, although a tad too enthusiastic. Her scent was…too citrus. "You look nice, Stace." It's *my* running joke. I plan to fuck her on their wedding night.

She blushes and smiles, putting her hand closer to mine and trying for a sexy look, stupid cunt. It's what Peter deserves though. He's an asshole too.

I turn to the girl sitting next to her, a blonde with her hair up. She has big ears, but other than that she's good looking. "Would you like to dance?" I can see the look on Stacy's face is almost as crushed as the hopeful one on this girl's. The blonde nods and stands quickly.

I like to celebrate after a transaction. I like to fuck afterwards. After weeks or months of training a new product, I like to enjoy the simple pleasure of a fuckfest with a whore of my choosing. I look around as I take her hand and lead us to the center of the dance floor; I'll have my pick tonight.

"My name's Stacy too." She giggles. I hate girls that giggle. I have to unclench my fist against her back, wondering how her giggle would sound if stopped by a quick pop to her ribs. I smile more.

"Simon."

"Oh, I know. You probably don't remember…we went to Stanford together."

I keep my smile plastered in place. "Of course. How's your family doing?" I watch her face fall a little. I know who she is and that her family was involved in a few financial scams years back. I believe her brother may still be fighting in court to stay out of jail. That should keep her from giggling until I can get rid of her. Her perfume is disgusting up close.

I glide us around the floor, looking around for a better choice for my cock tonight. I may just leave here and go to a club. The anonymous route is always more my taste, and I can keep a lookout for my next product. I have an order for a tall brunette with no ink. That's harder to come by these days.

I spot a short brunette in a long red dress. I like red for the obvious reasons.

This one is bright red, no pretending it's trying for subtle or sophisticated. It's a fuck me color. And this girl's hair is a wild, kinky curled mass around her that covers her shoulders and obscures her profile, but her body is on full display. There's not much to her. She's a little too thin, too up and down, but I like how her hipbone sticks out. She's purposely standing to make her angles sharper, pushing her leg through the long slit. She clearly makes no apologies for her body, and she's owning the two men standing next to her. They're practically sitting on their hind legs for her.

Her head leans back with a laugh at something one of them said, and thank God it's not a fucking little girl giggle. It's full throat and moaning, like she just heard a dirty joke, and she's making it dirtier by laughing at it so openly. I imagine having my hand on her throat while she laughs like that.

I watch her own hand travel up her side and rest on her collarbone. I can't see her face, but I can see her arm angled out sharply and her talons glinting as she plays her fingers against her creamy skin. I can feel my cock twitch.

Congrats, Red. You're about to enjoy a night of pussy melting sex with yours truly. I thank Stacy and turn away from her before she can say anything. I just leave her on the floor. I'm known for being an asshole. It's a reputation I aim to keep, discreetly of course.

I circle around the red dress and head to the bar opposite her. I don't think I've fucked her before, but I don't usually go for seconds. It's too messy. The girl starts thinking she has a chance and then discretion is harder to maintain. I need to make sure before making a move.

I get a drink and turn to check her out more. I recognize both men by her sides. They're brothers, new money, small tech, and thankfully, not clients. One brother keeps lifting his hand to brush her back but then drops it just as quickly. She's only slightly angled closer to him, only slightly tilting her face more towards him. So they've fucked, but he knows he's not good enough for her. And so does she. Poor bastard.

Not for the first time, I think about the offer to teach a class. One of Grandfather's friends made a joke again over a card game a few months back, saying how he wished I could teach his grandson a thing or two about women. He's a client, so I know he was speaking more about the special training I give my girls. It's unfortunate some men just can't stomach the necessary steps it takes to make a good girl great.

I tilt my head back to finish my drink and spit some of it out when I get my first good look at Red's face. It's *her*. It's *fucking* her. She's here. How? What the *fuck*?!

I brush away the bartender's hand and towel. "I'm fine." I move away from the bar a little, getting closer to the small group.

It's definitely Grace. She has the same dark eyes, same lips, but she's no longer cold, no longer distant. Everything is different—her hair, clothes, makeup…the way she moves, stands, talks. She's a fucking cat ready to spring. Her eyes drag across the room and spot new prey.

I can just barely hear her at this distance. Even her voice is different. It's almost the same, but more…sultry. It's not a word I use, but it's all I can think. Her halting voice is now a purr, low and deep and smooth. I'm blown away.

I lost track of her fifteen months ago. She disappeared completely and never returned to her shitty apartment or job.

I had to scramble to find a new product, but I obsessed about her. I tried to find out anything I could about her. Discreetly. I came up with nothing.

I figured she was running from her past and bolted to a new destination and identity. Or she was one of the unidentified girls killed every day. Or she was on to me and she ran. Most likely, it was the second option.

But now she's here, looking like this, acting like this. Her. Here.

Seattle: Miles Vanderson

Time teaches hard lessons.

When Gillian first went missing, I was sure that she was kidnapped, taken against her will. The police, FBI, investigators were all convinced of the same thing. As far as everyone knew, my stepsister was a sweet, innocent girl caught up in a sadistic ransom plot. I made it well known that I would pay any price to have her returned to me safely. Rewards were offered and upped.

I was certain that Gillian wouldn't have left me of her own volition; but then no information came. There was no ransom, no demands, no leads. That was my first lesson, humility.

And that led to my education with the harder lessons of patience, perseverance, and composure. I learned quickly to not break down every time the phone rang or when another search along the many nearby waterways didn't produce any clues. When I heard "no news is good news" over and over or when enough time went by that the investigation shifted from ransom to runaway, I learned to maintain my equanimity.

I remained calm through the many questions about Gillian's home life, hobbies, and habits. I endured the countless inquiries about her friends and potential boyfriends, or really, the lack of both. I was composed even when the investigation delved into my personal life. I stayed tight-lipped when my staff and friends were pulled into it.

When the investigation stagnated quickly after the trail of money turned cold in Seattle, that's when the lessons were hardest.

Three long years I waited to hear from her, to hear about her. I held on to hope for a long time. I hoped that Gillian would come to her senses and return to me on her own. It was a final lesson in foolishness.

It's been three long years of not knowing, of keeping my mask of composure on, and hiding the rage I feel inside as it grows every day that she remains missing.

San Francisco: Simon Lamb

I watch Grace walk away from the brothers. She heads towards the doors but stops at the circle of men I saw her eyeing before. She's smart. These are better options—much older money, slightly older men. She picks the weakest and moves in. It's a good choice, I admit. She'd be at the top of the food chain quickly with him.

I follow at a distance, not within listening distance, but it's not something I need to hear. The conversation is obvious. Yes, I know I'm beautiful and fuckable. Yes, I know I'm rich and that's my best quality. Now, let's get down to when, where, and how much.

It's the same no matter who's doing the talking…girl's got pussy, how much are you willing to give out to get in it. Most bastards don't realize this until they're standing next to an altar. And they always wonder why the chick isn't as interested in sex afterwards. Because you already paid the Goddamn price of admission, dumbass!

Red. Grace. She's good. She's smooth. She doesn't linger. She hints. She suggests. But she moves on quickly.

Men need to hunt. She obviously understands this. She's offering herself as prey. Not easy prey. But willing.

Is this why she disappeared? I found her when she was only taking a break in between men?

No…no fucking way! She was a small, sheltered, little girl, frozen behind expressionless stares and never venturing to even touch another person. I watched her for almost four weeks. She never said more than a few words together unless it was about the fucking stars and alignment and astro-fuck-shit. No way she was only pretending, laying low.

I don't know *this* Grace though. This woman didn't exist fifteen months ago. Grace was smart, but she was weak, meek, and docile. She didn't stand out, and she didn't want to. I chose her because she stood out trying so hard *not* to. And *I* wanted her. I wanted to break through her indifferent stares.

I'd dropped off a product near the grocery store that time I first saw her. I'd gone in afterwards to pick up a bottle of champagne. I'd already text a fuck for the night, but then

I saw Grace and decided to keep an eye on her. I tracked her. She was undeniably a perfect fit for my training. I thought she'd be a small challenge, and she sort of fit a new order I had back then.

This woman? She's on a Goddamn stage. She doesn't have to do more than flick her hair a little to get noticed. She's unwavering, confident, and hot. She's fuck me at your own risk if you dare and if you can pay the price. She's definitely not suitable for my training. Well, maybe…except now she's in my circle. Sort of.

I watch her walk back to the brother. He's fucking trussed up dinner in her hands. She pats him on the back and walks away with both brothers trailing behind. I follow and watch her get in a limo outside. She's clearly fucked the driver before by the smile they share and maybe the brother? Or maybe she's only fucked *with* him?

I walk outside and take in the cold air. What the fuck?!

Grace. Here. Like this?! I can't get my head around it.

San Francisco: Simon Lamb

I wait for her outside her address. It's a step up from Chinatown, Grace. A doorman holds open the glass door for her, and she barely brushes her tits against him as she passes. It could've been an accident, but I can see the smug half smile on her face as she puts her sunglasses on. He's still checking out her ass.

She's in red again, a little more subtle this time. Everything about her is polished and expensive except her hair; it's still wild and kinky.

Her strides are long for her short legs. Heels clicking, ass shooting side to side—it's a runway walk. She's bony like a model. That's her job now, though she's too short to make it big. She has a few gigs with local boutiques, a photographer that specializes in soft porn for book covers, and a few legit magazine shoots.

I glance at my phone. I have a few pics with her dark hair straight and sleek. I prefer her like this though, like she's been pumped with electricity. I smile. I could get more than just her hair to stand up with a few volts.

Supposedly, fifteen months ago she was in the Riviera, sulking over a bad break up with some underwear model or local politician's boy. Maybe it was both if rumors were true.

But I know she was in that crappy Chinatown apartment, hiding. Why?

It doesn't matter. She's now off limits. So why am I still watching her?

It's pretty simple. No girl's ever gotten away from me.

San Francisco: Simon Lamb

I keep my distance, but Grace is easy to follow. I track her to a trendy fusion restaurant and watch her sit with three other overly thin women. I decide to wait at the bar; it's close enough to their table to overhear most of what she'd say.

It's not close enough to smell her though. I miss her smell. I kept one of her bras for a while, thinking I'd choke her with it when I found her again. I threw it away finally, giving up after six months of looking for her. That and the smell no longer was hers.

The conversation at her table is inane. It's all fashion, fashion shoots, and fashion fucks; but her voice stays low, deep. Her laugh is the same from last night—hard, strong…sultry. The other women whine and giggle, trying to outshine each other. Grace is steady, smooth. It's almost like she knows she's being watched, and she's trying to be extra sexy while coming across like she's not trying at all.

I glance again in her direction. No, I'd bet my reputation as a top producer of fuck toys that she has no idea she's being watched.

I tune out their words, pulling out my phone to look over investments, catch up on emails. I even text my cousin about his visit next week. I occupy my mind with the mindless shit of life.

I get up and throw extra money on the counter without waiting for the bill when I hear the women divvying up their check.

Keeping my back to the door of the restaurant, I wait across the street but with a clear sightline of her through a reflection on a storefront window. I move with Grace as she walks but keep traffic and tourists between us. She heads into a small shop with the other women.

I plan, I'm meticulous, but I'm also a man of impulse and have learned to trust my inner voice too, my gut. I don't have a plan with Grace anymore anyway, so what the hell?

I cross the street quickly, ignoring the honk from oncoming traffic. I enter the low-music, leather smelling store. Great. Shoes. Women's shoes. Hard to look inconspicuous in here.

Fuck it.

"Those will make your feet look big." I stand right next to Grace, tall against her short frame. I actually look down my nose at her. Her startled look is quick to disappear. She's composed by the time she drags her eyes up my body. I have an urge to swallow under her gaze. Nicely done, Grace.

"Oh? Maybe that's what I'm going for."

I laugh, "Some men *do* have a foot fetish. Usually for the small variety though."

"Some men? Or you?" She hasn't moved, still holding the heel in her right hand. She hasn't tried to put any distance between us. She's all confidence and poise. Just as I start to answer, she interrupts, taking my eyes with hers back down her skin-tight jeans. "And I know I have nice feet." She lifts her head a little, not quite smiling with her lips, only her eyes. "*You* like them, don't you?"

I give her a full wolfish smile, all teeth. Still, there's no shaking her confidence. "Take off your shoes." I'm hard. I'm not a foot guy. I've had a few as clients, and I've tried to understand the whole fetish shit. But this is the first we've spoken; this is the first order I've given Grace.

No change to her face or body, and with hardly any movement at all, she slowly takes her feet, one at a time, out of her shoes. She stays on tiptoes for a moment longer, dark eyes still locked on mine. I watch her inch lower, gracefully, down to her natural height.

I can't get over how different she is. I'd swear she's a twin, a yin and yang, except I know this *is* the same girl. Even her smell is different though. It's deeper, stronger, like her voice. It's still clean, but now there's a hint of something earthier, richer. I can't put a name to it, but it's nice. It's still all her, no disgusting fake perfume.

I give her a slow, smooth charm smile this time, knowing it makes me more handsome, my blue eyes more striking. I've been told this my whole life. I let my eyes take their time traveling back down her body, all else forgotten. "You *do* have nice feet." She responds with a small frown to her perfect brows, and I'm pleased to see her skin's not frozen by injections. She's young, but that doesn't stop most of the girls in her line of work from overdoing the plastic shit. I enjoy seeing the full extent of emotion on a woman's face, especially pain. "We should go somewhere more private, though, before I tell you to remove anything else."

Her laugh is the same as yesterday—rich, long, deep. Her head is thrown back, lips full and open, teeth parted, and pink tongue on display. She's not faking this laugh. There's no forced effort, no attempt to make it more feminine or lighter. She tosses the shoe in her hand onto an empty chair and moves her hand to squeeze her own throat. She touches her laugh just the way I want to.

I wait for her to quiet, for her friends to come in closer to see what's so funny. They're piranha circling fresh meat. I give each a tooth-filled smile before landing my stare on her again.

She finally steps back to get a good look at me. I know what she sees. I'm tall at 6'3", in very good shape, muscled and lean. It's easy to see this, even in a coat. I'm casual, but there's my watch, my shoes; I obviously have money. I could be a model but her direct opposite—my light blond to her deep chestnut, my ice blue to her rich chocolate. Clean cut and all American, I look innocent and sweet, impish and charming. I've been told all this by countless women who learn how wrong they are very quickly.

I give her time to think these thoughts, watching her face play with each one. I answer her friend's questions while keeping my eyes locked on hers. "No, I followed her in here to see if her voice is as nice as her ass." The friends laugh, but she doesn't. Her eyebrow makes a perfect arch, her hand still languidly tracing the line of her neck as she decides what to make of me. She's enjoying watching me track her tiny movements. She's used to controlling a man's hunger for her, feeding it. She likes pulling the strings.

"And?"

"Turn around." She smiles at my second order, but she slowly rises back onto her toes and puts one foot in front of the other before turning slowly, lazily, around to stop with her ass to me. "Nice." Giggles and jokes from the friends, but she only turns just as slowly to stop in front of me again with a slight smile fluttering her lips.

I glance at my watch. "It's early, but let's grab a drink." I purposely don't include her friends in my look.

She gives me a full smile this time. "Only if you help me on with my shoes again." She lifts one foot and circles it from her ankle, stopping with pointed toes out to me.

I grin and lower onto one knee, grabbing her right calf and foot firmly. She places just the tips of her fingers to steady herself against my shoulder. Delicate but not tentative, she's sure of herself. She's almost laughing again at me, on bended knee to her.

I only smile back, watching her red toenails disappear into the heel. When I stand, I wrap my fingers around her thin arm, not pulling, not squeezing, just making it clear that we're leaving together now. She seductively blinks through her thick dark lashes up at me, a smile coiling her lips into a grin. She foolishly thinks she's still in control, that she ever was.

"Bye, girls," she tosses over her shoulder, allowing me to guide her out of the store and back onto the street. Giggles are thankfully lost behind the closed door. "So, where shall we go for this drink?"

"Around the corner there's a good place." I continue to pull her along but keep at her pace. I like the feel of her body strutting next to me; I don't want to throw off her rhythm. Her firm steps click away on the pavement, causing her body to brush against mine with every other step. On purpose or not, it's nice.

I still don't have a plan. I should be heading in the opposite direction. This was a woman I was thinking to take and torture before selling her off. Walking with her, like this, I'm on unfamiliar ground. Maybe I just need to fuck her to get her out of my system, to stop obsessing, and forget about her. Maybe.

"I suppose I should be asking your name, who you are, what you do?" She smiles, relaxing into the curve of the plush booth more and tucking her bare feet up under her ass. She leans a little more towards me, a little more into the table. "But I sort of like the mystery…so don't tell me. Let me guess."

"All right, but then it's my turn to guess about you." I smile, but I'm not sure about this. I can't reveal too much of myself or of what I know about her. No, this will be a one-time thing. Fuck and forget. I relax more with this thought. I watch the ice tumble and slip in my glass as I lift it to my lips.

"Hmm. You are free during the afternoon on a usual workday. So, I'm thinking you're in finance…stocks, bonds, that sort of thing?" I shake my head, and she exaggerates a pout and frown in response. Her skin glows in the low light; her dark eyes are black shiny stones. "Maybe a business owner, the boss blowing off his busy schedule to stalk unsuspecting women?" I laugh but shake my head again. Close, but I'm not going to say that. "Hmm. A doctor? Lawyer?"

She reaches out and grabs my hand suddenly. A firm and strong grip, she flips it over to look at my palm. Her touch is cool, fingers delicate, but she rubs hard against a worn spot. "Well you do *some* work with your hands...an engineer?" The callous came from using a small chain to whip my last product. I smile, making a mental note to pick up a new pair of leather gloves before I find my next girl.

I shake my head again. "What's the matter? Can't you read palms?" This is maybe a little close to her astrology shit, but I can't help teasing her.

She narrows her eyes and drops my hand onto the table. "Please tell me you're not a model!"

I laugh loudly at this. "No, trust fund baby. I do nothing to earn the millions I have to play with."

She raises an eyebrow. "Hmm. Only millions?" She tilts her own drink back and swallows the rest in one gulp, elongating her neck to enjoy its slow travel down her throat. I watch her swallow and again have to resist the urge to grab her throat. She gets the waiter's attention easily and orders two more drinks. I was surprised the first time when he didn't card her, but it's quiet and dark in here. I also gave him a tip already for showing us to the quietest and darkest booth.

"You sure you can handle another one?" She only smiles in response, the same quirking of coiled lips around a secret.

She moves her hands, languidly, to caress herself often. Her fingers glide through her mass of hair, down her neck, up her arm. She knows the effect; she knows I'll follow along, look where she wants me to. "Your turn."

I lean back, watching her down half the new drink in one long sip. "You're out shopping in the middle of a workday, so not an office job." She shakes her head with a bigger smile. "No books, so not a student." She shakes again, fingers trailing across the top of her chest. "Pretty. Nicely dressed." She smiles wider again at the small compliments, tilting her chin up, so the light can highlight her cheekbones more. "Too thin." She frowns, genuine this time. "*You* must be a model."

She raises her glass to me but doesn't smile. "Too thin?"

I lean in. "Like you'd be too easy to break."

Her smile is more than playful this time; there's no hiding the wicked spark in her eyes to my obvious challenge. "And you'd be the first man that didn't want a woman to be easily broken?"

I laugh, leaning back and finishing my drink as she does hers. "Not *easily*. Where's the fun in that?"

"One more?" She turns for the waiter before I even reply.

"You are *too* thin to drink like this." I lower my voice, adding a little of the natural authority I have to it.

"I don't get drunk." For just a second, it's her blank stare—eyes dead, face frozen. It's the Grace I knew in Chinatown but in this pretty costume.

"We'll see about that."

She surprises me by not responding submissively to my obvious deep, commanding tone. She laughs, eyes lit once more, face back to the mask of seduction. Looking at her mischievous grin and fluttering lashes, this time I do reach out. I put my hand right on her shoulder, my thumb rubbing up and down the side of her neck. She doesn't pull back, not right away. She only laughs at me a little more, leaning into my hand for one moment.

When she does move, it's quick and smooth. Her shoulder turns, hair feathering over my arm as she leans back. "Don't you think I should know your name if you're going to be touching me like that?"

"No."

"And you don't want to know *my* name?"

"No."

"Hmm. Then I shall call you Trust, trust fund boy."

"And I'll call you Red."

She smiles at this, almost a shy smile; her voice softens a little. "As good as any name I've been called."

The waiter arrives with the drinks, and she doesn't hesitate. She gulps hers down in one tilt of her head, eyes shining at me in challenge, all softness gone again. I toss mine down too. I'm going to be carrying her out of here.

Standing again on the street with the fog creeping in, I put my arm around her waist, pulling her towards me. It's getting dark already, a cold gray sky barely lit against the tops of buildings. She moves out of my arm quickly and saunters to the curb, hailing a cab. She ignores the glares from a group of business men when she easily steals what should've been their ride.

I open the door and she smiles at me, sliding over the seat but only part way. She presses her legs against mine. She's not even a little tipsy. She matched me drink for drink with no slurring, no sloppy silly girlishness, no change.

"Are you Russian?" I'm laughing, brushing my hand through her hair as I turn to her more.

She turns her body to me too and laughs with me. "I don't think so. I suppose I could be. Why?" I like the way her spicy scent mixes with the vodka. She leans a little more onto me, her hand flat and pressed against my chest. She lowers her voice and adds an accent, "Would Boris like a naughty Natasha in his bed?"

I press us together with my arm behind her as the rocking from the cab's shot suspension keeps her tits bumping against me nicely. Her lips are wet and apart, just waiting for mine, her eyes half-open and head tilted perfectly to the side. I smile at how easily we fit together, how she anticipates me. The tip of her pink tongue meets mine before our lips are even sealed. She lets out a small moan as my tongue moves around hers in a lazy dance. I grab her throat again. I'm gentle, not using much pressure, but her moan increases, vibrates under my fingertips. Her own hand rakes through my hair, pulling slightly in the back.

Her eyes are bright and shining when I finally release her. She runs her finger along her lower lip, smiling at me. It's an obvious invitation to kiss her again that I can't refuse.

I open the door and let her walk in first. Entering my main room, the surrounding city lights are enough to see the shape of my furniture profiled against the tall windows. I leave my lights off but turn to her quickly.

She surprises me by sidestepping at the last second, walking farther into the room. I take off my coat and unbutton my shirt, yanking it free from my jeans. She's turned around to watch me, hands on her hips. Her tiny frame topped with her mass of hair is only a dark shape against the windows. Her face is completely masked in shadow. "Take off your coat, Red."

She moves slowly to shrug out of her jacket. Her shirt and jeans are tightly formed to her bony shape. I watch her take her top off over her head and can see that she wasn't wearing a bra. She turns a little to toss her shirt onto a chair. It's a deliberately seductive motion. Putting her hands on her hips, slowing as she turns back to me, the light behind her shows off her erect nipples and perky tits for a moment longer.

Her head nods towards me. "Tit for tat, Trust."

I grin and remove my shirt and jeans, letting them drop with my underwear to the floor. I know my body is easier to view in this light. I know she can almost fully see the muscles of my chest and stomach, the hard ridges on my arms and shoulders, the strength of my thighs. And my big cock, of course. I'm not fully hard, but I'm getting there.

She doesn't wait for my command but does an unhurried job of undoing and lowering her jeans. Turning again to the side, she puts her ass in the air, upper body bending down the full length of her straight legs. Her small tits and hard nipples hang down, begging to be pinched and pulled. She pops her head up quickly, keeping her back arched and tits out. With a fake, helpless voice, "Looks like I'll need some help getting my shoes *off* this time."

I close the distance between us and put my hand out for her to hold, but she shakes her head, her voice huskier, "On your knees, Trust."

I laugh. "Red, that was a one-time thing." She starts to shake her head again, but I put my hand between her tits and shove her hard backwards. She doesn't let out a sound as she drops onto the sofa. I grab both shoes and toss them, then yank off her jeans in one tug. She's laughing again, sprawled out for me—legs spread, arms wide. She has no shame. She knows she's beautiful.

I smile seeing her pussy waxed clean. Her lips are on full display. Her tight round cheeks are off the edge of the sofa. I lower to my knees, and she places her legs over my shoulders, smiling at me. "Knew I'd get you on your knees." I slap her thigh, not too hard, more playful but with a nice smack to it. She yelps teasingly and tilts her hips up towards my face.

"Ask nicely." I grip her thighs, liking how her muscles fight against the strength of my hands.

"Please!" She bites her lower lip, keeping it cinched under her white teeth, watching me and flaunting her pussy with a small pumping motion. I can feel her thighs tense more against me; her stomach is flat and muscled. "Pretty please!"

I slowly lower my face to her right thigh, kissing and licking my way towards her pussy. Her skin is silky and sweet tasting. Her hands reach for the sides of my head, but I lift my face. "No. Hands off." She pouts and smiles at the same time, dramatically raising hands over head to grasp the top of the sofa. I continue my kisses up and over the top of her smooth skin. I smile when she tries to grind against my mouth as I head back down her left thigh.

"Tease!" It's a fake whine, but it's filled with lust.

"You weren't specific, Red. You'll have to ask nicely to get exactly what you want." I flash a wicked grin, keeping my lips pressed to her leg, nibbling her thigh slightly. I have to laugh at the frustrated narrowing of her eyes though.

"Then by all means, I'll be very specific for you. Please place your mouth on my pussy, licking every inch you can reach with your beautiful tongue." I start to head towards her pussy again, but she stops me, "Wait…I'm not finished." I smile and raise my eyebrows. "I want your tongue darting in and out of me fast, I want your tongue like a straw around my clit while you suck me deeply, and I want your tongue flat and hard against me like I'm the best fucking ice cream you've ever tasted, Trust."

I smile, impressed with her. Most women are too shy to talk this way, even with a guy they know. Grace has no such limitations. "Yes, ma'am." I lower my lips to cup over her pussy, pulling the smooth skin into my mouth. I'm rewarded with a small gasp from her. She's swollen and wet already, turned on by her own words. I glance up and her head is pushed back, eyes closed. I let myself get lost in her.

My tongue works perfectly through all of the acrobatics she wanted, adding a few of my own. I stop her orgasm twice, though, forcing her to hold on a little longer despite her attempts to push against me, to move her hips to fuck my mouth. She's small, but strong. Her gasps and moans are getting stronger too. Finally, she lets out one long and loud, "Please." It's a plea full of need and frustration, her head shaking side to side against her upstretched arms.

I pull her off the sofa a little more, cupping her ass with both my hands. I've been ready for her, almost painfully hard. Keeping her legs on my shoulders, I push my cock to just inside her wet lips. "Is this what you want?" I won't be able to tease her for long; my own need is getting to be too much.

"Yes!" She pushes against me and the sofa at the same time, forcing more of me inside her. She's being a very greedy girl, but I can't pull back now. I squeeze her ass, stretching her apart more and slamming into her with all the need I feel—with all the need I've felt since I first saw her. She screams out and grinds against me. I can feel her tightness around me. I'm pushing against her, forcing my way inside her deeper, but she bucks and continues grinding hard.

We fuck each other—her pushing against the sofa, me pulling her to me. When she comes, it's in waves that squeeze my cock and force my own orgasm to stretch longer. My deep moan drowns out her long cry and final soft mewing.

I stop pushing against her but keep her legs pinned to me. When I open my eyes, hers are already smiling at me, her lower lip locked in her teeth again. I kiss both her thighs before gently lowering her legs to the floor. She stands, brushing her hair back as I kiss her stomach. "Bathroom's back there." I nod with my chin toward the hallway.

She saunters away, leaving her clothes on the floor. I watch her ass roll and hips shoot out. She has a great walk. I put on my boxers and head to the kitchen for a bottle of water. I come back to sit on the sofa like she was, slouched. She returns with a smile on her face and takes the bottle from me. I watch her neck move with big gulps of the cold water.

Her fearlessness, owning her nakedness even after sex, is beautiful to me. She can see me looking her up and down, and she obviously likes it. She hands me back the bottle. "Sorry, Trust, don't have time for seconds." She moves away from me before I can grab her.

I idly watch her pick up her clothes to get dressed when I have a thought. "Do you always leave the house without underwear?"

"I like to be unencumbered." She leans over and kisses my chest, her eyes hooded with thick lashes, her grin disappearing. "And I like the rough feel of denim against my pussy. Even more after rough sex."

I harden a little at her words. I grab her arm but allow her to pull away. "You don't want to stay longer? Order food, fuck some more?"

She smiles, pulling her top down and bending over in front of me to fluff her hair upside down. She has her jeans and heels on again too. Her ass is hard and her legs lean. She whips her head back up and tosses her hair side to side, not turning to me. "You're sweet, but my boyfriend will be home soon. I need to go."

I laugh. I want to see how far she's going to go with this. We still haven't exchanged names. She hasn't asked anything more about me. "So, how do I get in touch with you?"

She grabs her jacket and purse, turning to smile at me again from the door. "Is this really your place?" I nod. "Then I guess I know where to reach you if I'm in the mood for some ice cream again." Then she blows me a kiss before walking out my door.

I stand up, walking back into my kitchen. I don't keep much food stocked. I don't spend a lot of time here. Being in the city doesn't provide enough privacy for me or enough space. Torturing good screams out of a girl takes elbow room. A whip needs its length to really crack a good cry from eyes bled dry of tears already.

I stand in the cold air and light of the fridge, downing what's left of a jug of orange juice. Grace drained me in more ways than one. I wanted to be done with her, but she's sticking. I keep going back to the two versions of her I know—both cold, both distant. Both are beyond my reach in a way.

I'm not vain. Narcissistic, sure, but everyone confuses these two. It's not vanity that has me wondering why she was so willing to come here, fuck me, then leave without even getting my name. I wonder because it's what I'd do.

She acted like me—in it only for her own reasons, not giving a shit about me.

I smile. That's why she's sticking? It's not the crazy shit of whatever she was doing in Chinatown. No, it's because today, she was like me. But is she? Really?

I want to know.

I smile. I want to have her. Fuck my rule.

San Francisco: Simon Lamb

The thing about an obsession is it takes a lot of energy and time. I think Ugo Betti said it best, "'Mad' is a term we use to describe a man who is obsessed with one idea and nothing else." I was told I have obsessive behavioral traits. Then I looked up everything to do with obsession. I told the fucking shrink to kiss my ass after I learned the most brilliant minds are always obsessed with something.

It was Grandfather's doing, the shrink. He felt it was necessary after that first girl killed herself—after he learned what I'd done to her. Truthfully, he never understood me, but he tried his best to be a father to me. I did my best to make him think it was enough.

Now I find myself obsessed again. It's not my usual obsession either. *That* I can handle. Finding a new product, finding a way to break down a girl's resistance, finding a way to build her back up to an obedient singularity, finding a way to not be bored with doing all of the above—*that* I'm used to.

No, my new obsession has been to find out everything I can about Grace. And I am going mad with failing. I have only come up with a paltry sum of details.

The Chinatown apartment is still rented under her name. All her things are still there. The food is long rotted in the fridge, dust collected on her clothes and bed, but rent is paid automatically each month. She never went back to the twink store, never collected any of the astrology shit she left behind.

The queens who treated her like family said they received an email telling them she went back home, but they didn't know where that was. They both had tears describing how distraught they were at her abrupt leaving and her rudeness for not staying in contact. It was easy to get them to talk. I acted in need of a good horoscope reading for my best chances to meet Mr. Right. They referred me to a place down the street since they didn't have the heart to hire anyone to take Grace's place.

They have no idea that she is still in the city or that she has a one-bedroom condo in Potrero too. It's small, a second floor unit, bright and cheery. All her clothes in the closet are bright and cheery. It's the antithesis of the Chinatown apartment. The only similarity is the art; it's all framed children's drawings. She hasn't been there in months. A cleaning service keeps it all neat and tidy for her in case she ever returns. It still smells like her at least, like she might be back at any minute.

She lives with her boyfriend full-time now. That's the building I saw her leaving. There's not much of her in his apartment, though, except the mess of clothes, makeup, and jewelry she leaves lying around. The rest of the apartment is a typical guy place—black leather, big TV, nothing changed by a feminine touch.

She lives there but still out of a suitcase, just a bag tossed in the corner and forgotten. Her things are all scattered like they don't really have a home. Half the closet is emptied. Poor bastard, he'd tried to make room for her, invite her in. She never took over the space.

Two years ago she became the girlfriend to a photographer. It didn't last, but he got her pictures to the right people, got her started in her low-rate modeling career. Two years ago was the start of both the lease in Chinatown and the purchase of the Potrero condo. It was like she knew she'd need both sooner or later.

But before two years ago, she didn't exist. She has no connection with anyone—no family, no friends, no online presence, no credit history. Her SSN is a clean slate until two years ago as well. She paid cash for her condo, paid in full. She still doesn't have any credit history. There are no credit cards, no investments, just a bank account.

She has a security deposit box too—boxes, actually—but not even I can get into those.

I couldn't find anything out about her before two years ago. She didn't exist before then. No birthplace, no details, not even a driver's license or ID to be found.

So I'm back to my theories, but each one is more farfetched than the last. Runaway from a crazy husband? Witness protection? Fugitive? Each one only explains so much, then falls apart.

And I am going mad with obsession now. I'd meant to get information, and then use it to seduce her, win her, dump her. I wanted to get rid of her once and for all—purge her.

But now I'm obsessed.

I know only one surefire cure for what obsesses me.

San Francisco: Simon Lamb

"Simon, are we going out tonight or not?!"

I flip back to the game, drowning out any other noise with the volume of the crowd cheering and announcers yelling about the upset. Sweet. I just won some cash and my fantasy football league for the week. I click the TV off and stand up, stretching as I say, "Fine, cry baby. We can go out."

Cary throws his empty beer bottle at me; it thuds against my leg and falls to the rug, spinning. "Fucker."

I leave the bottle; that's what a maid's for. I walk down the short hall to my room but yell back at my cousin, "Get dressed. I'm not taking you anywhere if you still have on that fucking ripped t-shirt." I can hear him laughing and being a smartass, but he's being quiet about it. I can also hear him heading to the other room. He knows how far he can push me and when to just shut up and do as he's told.

I grab a quick shower and dress in my usual club crawl uniform—button-down, jacket, jeans, no socks, loafers. It's casual but nice; I don't have to say I have money. I don't have to convince anyone that I'm good looking; I don't have to try too hard to get what I want. I just am; I just do.

Cary is standing in the kitchen, finishing the last of another beer. He has on a similar uniform but with a non-ripped t-shirt under his jacket. "Come on. We'll grab dinner before hitting a club." He nods. He's always up for whatever I want to do. It's one of the things I love best about him.

He's younger than me but not by much. We look alike. The biggest difference between us, besides my money, is his upbringing. He had the benefit, or disadvantage, of both his parents living. They weren't together, at least not since he turned eight, but both his parents are alive and kicking. His father and mine were brothers. I suppose in some ways he should be jealous of me. His father certainly is.

I inherited all of Grandfather's money. I was his sole heir, but I was also his second chance to get it right. And he did try. In the end, the best Grandfather could do was give me his millions…and a long letter. He tried to leave a lasting impression with words of wisdom. I still have the letter. I read it on my birthday every year, just in case I get something out of it after all this time. It's the least I can do for him.

Cary's never acted jealous though. We spent most summers together, along with his sister, Sophia. They are the closest thing to family I know, and I've been generous with both of them. I've paid for colleges, houses, vacations, cars, lawyers, whatever. I've paid to keep their names out of headlines or in them, however the case may be, and they've

been loyal to me since childhood.

"Her?" I shake my head. Cary looks frustrated again. He sips his drink and scans the lower level of the club once more. "What about the short brunette there?" He nods towards a corner of the dance floor below us.

I turn quickly at his description. It's not Grace. And I'm angry for hoping that it would be. "We're looking for whores, not cheerleaders, Cary!" I down my drink and leave it on the small ledge. "My turn."

I scan the crowd and easily spot a few options. "Come on." I lead us down the stairs and into the thick of people. I usually hate crowds. I hate the press of other people on me, but clubs are different. Maybe it's the lights or the music. Maybe it's the smell—alcohol and sweat. With the lack of clothes, limbs grind and fly, slamming bodies together and tossing pheromones around.

I get off on the hunting—looking around and spotting the perfect prey, slowly circling and examining, watching her posture for me. I have wondered why women are so stupid though. I haven't had this thought in a long time, I think because I'd given up caring altogether, but tonight I'm back to it as Cary and I buy drinks for two girls I spotted.

I wonder if they see the looks we're giving them, giving each other. Don't they smell the danger they're in? Don't they recognize a predator? Has womankind evolved too far past the primitive to be able to decipher the subtle clues of hunter and hunted?

This brings my thoughts around to Grace again. I've not stopped thinking about her. She understood about hunting. She was aware that she was prey; she thrived on it. But it was deceptive with her. She was just as much the hunter as I was. She was playing her own game for her own thrills, and I admired her for it.

She wasn't like these girls. She didn't believe any of my bullshit or try to get me to be her Prince Charming. She got what she wanted; then she was through with me. I have to stop thinking about her! Tonight is about having fun, not thinking about business or her or any other damn thing.

I give a big wolfish smile to the girl on my right. She's taller than Grace. Her light brown hair is smoothly straightened and cut chin length. Her eyes are an indefinable color in the low light. Green maybe? She's cute. She doesn't giggle at least but keeps her laugh inside, only shaking with it. Or maybe it's just too quiet to hear over the loud music and people.

I lean over to her ear and whisper, "I like your laugh." I bite her neck before moving away. It's a good test. She only puts her hand to the spot and laughs again. I can't help thinking that Grace would've had a good come back. At the very least, she would've taken her own bite out of me. I smile again with this thought. This girl thinks it's because of her, and she smiles even more at me, swaying side to side. Her name is Maria or Mary…something like that.

I signal to Cary that it's time to move things along. He nods and asks the tall blonde he's leaning against if she'd like to join us in the VIP section. Of course she says yes. I don't wait for her to ask her friend. I grab the waist of my girl and push her to follow in their direction.

I'm pissed by the time we hit the hotel. Both girls are trashed and so is Cary. Hell, so am I, just not as much as everyone else. I never bring girls back to my place, not club girls anyway—too messy to get rid of, not enough privacy. I always arrange a hotel suite when Cary is in town so we can have fun without fucking up my life.

If I'm honest, I started tonight off pissed, and now I'm even more pissed. Maria, Mary—whatever the fuck her name is—can't even hardly talk, let alone fuck. She seemed fine at the club, but in the cab ride over, her head started drooping. She threw herself on top of me, and her body was like dead weight. She's even sloppier now that we're inside the room.

Cary shrugs his shoulders at her prone body on the suite's sofa. He knows that I don't go for a dead fuck. If a girl can't even keep her eyes open, I see no point in having sex with her. I know there are plenty of guys that would take advantage of this situation, but I need a conscious girl to have fun. He tilts his head towards his girl, his eyebrows raised in question.

We've shared before. I shrug back. I'm not in the mood to share. I'm not in the mood to be in this situation at all. I'm fucking thrown off my fucking game. My bad mood is starting to become a really bad mood. I turn away from him so he can't see my anger.

It's all Grace's fault. I haven't been able to clear her out of my head. I'm stuck on her, obsessed with all I don't know about her and the little I do. Fuck. I need to stop. Now.

I turn around with a forced sense of calm. Cary is slow dancing, undressing the other girl. She's pretty. She and Cary make a nice pair—dark blond against lighter blonde. She's skinny, but her ass is a little big for her shape, just Cary's type.

Her back is to me, so she's either forgotten that I'm in the room or she doesn't care that I'm watching him undress her. His lips trail over her shoulder, his eyes on me. Asshole has to stop himself from laughing. I roll my eyes. I know he's waiting to see what I want to do.

We've found that it's easier to get a girl to go along earlier rather than later in the proceedings. I shrug again and move closer to them, undoing my shirt. Cary pushes her bra straps down and she takes her arms out of them, hugging him close around his neck. He has her short skirt unbuttoned just as I gently stroke her back.

She lets out a little startled cry, realizing that I'm close and touching her too. Her head leans back into my chest, and her eyes are wide as they look up at me. I stop her from saying anything, cupping her chin and forcing her head back a little more as I kiss her. She kisses me back, a good sign. I can feel her moving as Cary forces her skirt and underwear down. With my free hand, I release her bra and it falls to the floor.

I pull back, letting go of her mouth but not her chin. My free hand moves down her side, making her shiver against us. Her eyes stay watching me. I reach her hip and pull her to me, pushing my erection into her back. Cary runs his tongue over her stretched neck and she moans, closing her eyes.

Her eyes pop open when he bites her nipple a little too hard, and I grab her ass at the same time. She opens her mouth, and I stop her again with a kiss. She pushes against Cary, into me, fighting to free her mouth this time. I pull back a little, and her lips brush mine with her words, "I can't do this," but she's panting. Cary has his hand between her legs already. Her protest is weak. I don't answer, just keep her head pinned back and squeeze her ass, stretching her open for him. Her pants turn to moans quickly.

"We'll take good care of you. I promise." My words are more whispers into her neck, against her shoulder, while Cary kisses her other side. "Do you want him to stop?" She shakes her head, moaning louder. "Be a good girl and answer me."

She moans a long, "No."

I let go of her chin, but she stays leaning against my chest. Cary's still kissing her neck and rubbing her pussy. I grab her hips from behind, pulling her hard against me, causing her to gasp again. Cary stops touching her and stands back a little. I turn her around to face me.

She's scared, uncertain, as she looks up my full height, but she wanted me in the beginning. I could tell. I went for the friend since I knew she was more Cary's type. That and her friend reminded me vaguely of Grace.

The thought of Grace has me pissed again. I push this girl down onto her knees harder than I need to, but she doesn't try to move away. I unzip my pants and pull out my cock. Her mouth is on me before I have my hand around her head.

Her tongue is nice, long and quick, but she only takes a third of me in her mouth. I close my eyes for a while, letting her face pump my cock. I'm not ready to come yet though.

I open my eyes and grin at Cary; he moves to stand next to me. I push her head off me and towards his cock. She looks up at him, and he smiles. She takes his cock in her mouth but looks at me.

I move over to the sofa, watching. Her drunk friend is passed out on the other end still, not even moving when I sit down. Cary tilts his head back, both hands on her head. I watch her suck him, her head bobbing quickly against him. She's not great, but she is enthusiastic at least.

Cary pulls her hair, and she lets go of his cock, looking scared again up at him. He keeps his hand in her hair and has her walk on her knees over to me. She frowns and pouts, but I can see that the humiliation turns her on more. He puts her face down towards my lap, and she pulls my cock into her mouth, her ass up in the air. She pauses, though, to turn her head back to him as he kneels and positions himself behind her. "I don't do anal. Okay?"

Cary slaps her ass and slams his dick into her wet cunt as his answer. She pushes against me with the force and grunts her pleasure. I grab her hair and yank her face back to me. She smiles as Cary slams into her again, moaning with her eyes closing as her mouth wraps around me.

I grin at Cary. I'll have to concentrate to come before him. Most girls don't like to continue giving head after they've come. Timing is everything as they say.

I close my eyes. The image of Grace sprawled out on my sofa comes to mind. I imagine my mouth on her while she sat like I am now—the sweet taste of Grace, her moans, her words, her spicy scent.

I push the blonde's mouth deeper on me, and she sucks harder. I can feel Cary pushing her. Her tongue works faster, and her hand strokes harder while he pumps into her. Finally, I hold her in place while I shoot come down her throat, imagining Grace the whole time. Cary has her screaming as I pull away from her, his own low groans quickly following. Timing.

Yawning and scratching the nail marks on my shoulder, I move into the kitchen for coffee, passing Cary at the table. I avoid looking at him, just grab a bowl and sit down to pour some cereal and milk. We eat in silence for a while.

We left the blonde and her friend in the hotel late last night. I glance at the clock on the microwave. They should just be getting the room service I ordered for them, unless they got up early and took the $20 I left for a cab already.

The three of us had a good time. Maria/Mary never did wake up to join in, but the blonde managed to keep us both happy a few more times. And her dislike of anal was a blatant lie. Or Cary is a better motivator than I thought. He's an ass man.

I can feel him watching me now. I know what he's thinking. I fucked up last night. I finally drop my spoon into the bowl, splashing milk and cereal out. "What?!"

He grins, one of his stupid looks. "Nothin, cuz." He's laughing though. Fucker.

"Cary." I growl his name through gritted teeth and shoot him another look of warning. He just gets up and walks to the sink with his bowl.

But he doesn't leave. I can feel him staring at me; I don't turn around. "So…who's Grace?" There's laughter in his voice still.

And the insane part? I hate hearing her name from his lips. I have an instant reaction of pure rage. I can feel my whole body tense, ready to spring up and thrash him. I have to close my eyes for a second to get it under control, to calm my voice. "Who?"

Cary moves around the table to stand on the other side, watching me. "You called the girl last night Grace."

I look up at him, still trying to get my body to relax. I'm not wearing a shirt, so the flexing of my arms and chest is clearly visible to him. I sit back, forcing my one hand to flatten on the table, the other to pick up the spoon again. I force a smile on my face too. "I must've been more shitfaced than I thought." But I can see that he's not going to let it go. "She was one of my products." That's not entirely a lie. She would've been.

He only nods but keeps watching me until I start eating again. Finally, he turns to leave. "I'm heading back. Call me when you have a new girl; I'll stop by to help out."

When I hear the bedroom door close, I let the spoon drop again. Fuck. I can't believe I let myself get so angry with him, all for mentioning her. This obsession is taking over.

I need to do something and soon. I can't let myself be preoccupied with Grace any longer. I have two orders waiting, and I haven't even tried to look for new girls.

For one moment, I think about grabbing Grace, taking her, training her and selling her off. It's what I'd planned before, what I told Cary I did already, but I can feel my body tensing at this thought.

I can lie to myself, say it's because she's off limits— my own stupid rules. But I know that's not it. Grace is only partially in my circle. She's a fucking model for fucksake, with absolutely no connections that I can find. She'd still be perfect to take, perfect to train, a perfect product for me.

Getting up and dumping my uneaten breakfast down the sink, I can feel myself tensing even more. So why the fuck can't I do it?!

It would end my obsession. Once I have her chained and broken, I know I'd be done with her. Except the thought sounds hollow to me now.

The longest I've ever been with one woman is seven months. She was the first girl, Raquel. I dumped her after she agreed to marry the man of her father's choosing. Well, to be fair, I was only sixteen. It wasn't like I was going to ask her to wait for me or anything. And I'd already had my fun with her by then, but that was the longest that I'd spent with one girl.

The girls I train usually only take a few weeks, a few months at the longest. Breaking a woman is easy once you apply simple mindfuck techniques. Lack of rest, sleep, food—these are the basics, plus equal applications of pain and comfort. The first few days are the hardest, getting to know fears and tolerance levels. Get them to eat from your hand and they're broken like any other animal. And I prefer to hand off ownership as soon after they're broken as possible; there's less confusion that way.

But Grace has been with me now for over sixteen months. I haven't had her physically for that time. She hasn't been chained in my cave the way I wanted. She hasn't been broken and trained for all that time. But I've thought about her, thought about what I would do to her. She *has* been mine, even if *she* didn't know it.

So now the thought of her being with anyone else, the thought of making her available to anyone else... I don't even want to finish the thoughts.

I want her broken. But *I* want her.

So now I have a plan again. This calms me.

Smiling as I head into my room, I think one more happy thought about her. Maybe I'll rename her. She'll be broken. She'll be anything I want her to be. Maybe I'll call her Scarlet.

San Francisco: Simon Lamb

I wait. I know she'll be here. I just wait for her. I've decided today is the day she comes to me. Willingly. Freely.

Or forcefully.

I don't care.

Today is the day, Grace. And *this* time, you're not getting away from me.

I look up each time the door opens. I reach for my cup of coffee each time it's not her.

Finally, I watch her enter the diner. Her hair's pulled back but still a mess of tangles and curls. Her face looks smaller left out in the open, her dark eyes even bigger. She's in her usual red. This time it's a tight pair of jeans, faded red. I watch her walk by the sign saying she should wait to be seated, as she always does. I smile, watching her sit at a table—same spot I've watched her take for four days.

I wait for the waitress to take her order before walking over. I wait until she's picked up the crayons and started coloring the paper placemat in front of her before walking over. It's her routine. She doodles until the waitress brings her food.

"Hello, Red."

She doesn't look up, not right away. Her shoulders come up, and her chin goes down. Her whole hand squeezes around the orange crayon, she breathes in three times rapidly through her nose, and she quickly drops the crayon, letting it roll off the table like I've caught her doing something wicked.

Then she relaxes, softens. Her eyes are the last part of her to raise to me. "Hello, Trust. How nice to see you again."

I don't sit down. I just lean over the booth. "Wanna join me for breakfast?"

She smiles. "Sure." She grabs her purse off the seat and slides towards me. "But if by breakfast you mean a quickie after pancakes, then I'm going to have to pass for now. Busy day."

I laugh. She's full of surprises. "Just breakfast, sweetheart." As she walks by me, I glance back down at her table. The placemat is full of jagged orange lines, like sunrays slashed across the center. It's not so much a doodle as random, angry lines.

Sitting back at my booth, I motion to the waitress that I'm ready to order. I can see that Grace keeps fidgeting with her hands on the edge of the table, bouncing her eyes from the small box of crayons and her placemat. Yet I've been told *I'm* obsessive?

"You want coffee, or have you already had too much?" I nod towards her hands.

She doesn't answer me, just looks up at the waitress. With a soft, almost girlish voice, higher pitched than her usual, "Milk...please?"

I laugh again as the waitress walks away. "Does a body good?"

"What?" Her expression is clouded.

"Milk?" I'm sarcastic, watching her fidgeting increase.

"Oh. Um. Yeah." She looks down at the napkin she's twisting and almost throws it to the edge of the table. She shakes her head, even lowers it a little for a moment. I just sit, frowning. Throwing her off routine really seems to do a number on her. Good to know.

I realize how little I actually know about her. I watched her for four weeks last year, but I learned almost nothing except that she likes her little rituals. She sticks to them religiously. We're alike in that way. I appreciate this about her.

She just doesn't know that I'm about to turn her little life upside down.

"Ya know, Trust…I'm sorry, but I just remembered..." And just like that, she jumps up and tries to get away. She nearly bumps into the waitress and topples the plates of food. She sits back down hard to avoid it.

As the plates are set in front of us, I can see that she's only getting more agitated, ready to run again. As the waitress walks away, I grab her hand from across the table and without letting go, I move to come over to her side. I force her to slide further into the booth and block her escape by sitting down.

"You okay?" I can add a lot of fake concern when I need to, but I *am* actually worried about her, a little anyway. She looks scared. I only want that look to be in her eyes when *I* put it there.

She takes one big breath, steadying again, but doesn't make eye contact with me. "Look. I don't mean to be rude..."

"So don't be." I add a little anger, just to see her reaction. It's not good. I was hoping for a quick backing down.

Instead, she turns to face me more, aggressive with her head cocked to the side and a half smile now on her face. "I was going to say that breakfast is sort of a ritual for me. I like to eat in peace." She leans in a little more. I can smell her spiciness mixing with the sweet pancake smell in here. It's making me want to dip her in syrup. "So, if you don't mind, we'll talk after I finish eating." But she ends with a small note of almost submission; her eyes drop down to her lap, voice getting softer, "Okay?"

I relax but stay sitting next to her. "Sure. I was taught not to talk with my mouth full anyway." She smiles and turns back to her plate of pancakes. I chuckle to myself seeing that they're the chocolate chip ones with whipped cream in the shape of a smiley face.

She transforms again, becoming completely focused on her plate. I have to stop myself from staring. She mumbles something before picking up her silverware. A prayer? You've got to be kidding me. She's religious? I didn't see that coming. I haven't seen any evidence of it before now.

She doesn't take her eyes off the plate, keeping her silverware firmly clutched in her fists. The only time she lets go is after every third bite, and that's to take the glass of milk with both hands to her lips. It's truly the strangest thing to watch. A ritual is right. I hope to shit she doesn't eat every meal like this.

When the glass of milk is gone, she pushes the plate away and sets the silverware down slowly. I have to stop from laughing again because the only part of the pancakes not eaten is the smiley face covered piece. "You know, you can order them without the whipped cream…"

It takes her a second to respond to me, like she was too deep in her own thoughts still. "Oh. Yeah. Maybe next time." As I pay the waitress, she looks down at her jacket and rolls her eyes at a dribble of syrup on it, mumbling, "Sloppy!" She dabs at it with a new napkin.

"You were pretty focused eating. I'm surprised anything could get away." I laugh openly at her this time.

She glares at me, still dabbing the spot. "What are you doing here? You don't live around here."

"No, but I met a client nearby." This is true. I've decided to put all new orders on hold for the time being, but this is an old friend, so I wanted to tell him in person. He wasn't happy about it, but what choice does he have really?

Her eyes narrow more at me, and she turns a little with that same aggressive cock to her head. "I thought you were a trust fund brat, all play, no work?"

"I am. The work I do is…more play…recreational." I grin at how true this is. "And I thought models lived on water and diet pills, not alcohol and pancakes."

"High metabolism, I guess." She purses her lips into a sarcastic grin. I'd like to smack her for it, but I settle on a mental list of behaviors to change. Top one right now is making faces at me, maybe followed by the weird eating habit. I'm still grinning, not letting her in on the joke just yet. She'll learn soon enough.

"So this has been fun, Trust, but I'll need to change now before heading out…" She's trying to push me out of the booth. I slide over and put my hand out to help her up again. She seems thrown by the simple gesture, hesitating and staring at my fingers.

My grandfather was a very gentlemanly old man. I know when to be, how to be; I just don't choose to be very often is all. I find it useful at times, though, especially when it's unexpected. It can really throw a girl off her game. It works on Grace.

As she takes my hand, I yank her firmly against my side. She tilts her head up, starts to close her eyes, and opens her mouth for the kiss she's already expecting. The pancakes make her lips even sweeter and her level of response, at least sexually, is good.

I grab her waist in a tighter grip with one arm and lead her towards the door. "Come on, I'll walk you out." She moves next to me, same as before—a cat strut, ready to pounce. I don't let go and she just keeps walking with me. I know we're heading back towards her boyfriend's apartment. I have no intention of letting her leave my side today.

Seattle: Miles Vanderson

Hanging up my cell phone, I head back to my chair next to the fireplace. I was reviewing financial statements and minutes from the board meeting when Spencer interrupted with his good news. Like my father, I still like to have reports printed. I prefer to feel them in my hands. It's just another way I know I'll never be free of his influence.

I toss the papers into the fire. I won't be able to concentrate on anything else tonight anyway. Leaning back into the wingchair more, I watch the fire dance and lick the edges of the papers, following the ashes as they float, the embers darkening. It's soothing for only a moment.

Spencer is "zeroing in on Gillian's whereabouts." He has a flare for the dramatic for a one-dimensional type. He's already impressed me with his tenacious gift for sifting through the information that his predecessors managed to mangle over the years. He's a real bloodhound with his tracking abilities, and he has Gillian's scent now. I could hear his excitement at the chase. The prize is within reach. I hope.

He found a coffee shop waitress at a hotel in San Francisco willing to swear it was Gillian whom she served breakfast. That was only a little over two years ago. She remembered Gillian's strange eating habits.

I smile remembering these too. Gillian is a unique girl, a broken into a million pieces girl. She's fragile and weak, intense and stubborn, lost and unbalanced, resilient and decisive. She's been my everything since the moment I first saw her.

I close my eyes to better picture her, just as she was that first time we met. It was in this very room, the library. It's why I spend so much time in here. It was Gillian's favorite room in this sprawling place. She said it was the dark, the feel of being surrounded and encased that she liked. I open my eyes for a moment, taking in the floor to ceiling shelves of books that no one reads, the panels of wood that add to the masculine, warm feel. It looks impressive; it looks like a library should. That's all that ever mattered to Martin Vanderson.

I close my eyes again and can almost hear Gillian against the crackle of the fire. I'd walked in on her crying soft sobs; she was sitting as close as she could to the fireplace on the rug. Her skinny legs were tucked up under her dress, her chin quivering and causing the tears to bounce over the thin material.

She was an angel, a dark angel against the orange flames. Her tiny face was illuminated yet shadowed, her dark eyes coal and ice, her tears the most beautiful sight I'd ever seen. She didn't startle; she didn't even react when I entered the room and came near her. She gave no sound or movement when I sat on this same chair behind her, keeping her silence as my own.

When she slowly twisted just her upper body to see me more and lifted her eyes that first time, I think I actually gasped. I know I drew my breath in. How could I not? She was perfection. The savage innocence in her eyes was undeniable.

I didn't move. I just sat still with my hands on my knees, much like I'm doing now, and waited for her to speak or move first. When she did, it was in a quick fluid motion. She stood, turned to me fully, and then stopped. Her face stayed in shadow, unreadable, but her small body was in perfect silhouette, projected by the fire behind her. The wispy ends of her hair were like the embers glowing. She stood with her legs slightly apart and her arms at her sides but open. It was like she was offering herself to me. She knew I could see her outline in full; the dress almost disappeared against the flickering light.

I groan even now picturing her. I will have that imagine emblazoned in my memory forever.

She stayed still long enough for my eyes to slowly travel up and down her body...twice. She was only starting to develop the shape of a woman. She was lean and muscled, soft and feminine, the briefest moment between mature angles and soft childhood captured in one body. I couldn't take my eyes away from her. I knew I should. I knew I should have broken the spell, but I didn't want to. So I didn't.

Then she walked the few steps towards me that it took to reach my chair. She lowered herself in one fluid movement again. She knelt at my feet and put her head against my knee, facing the fire once more. My fingertips were covered by her dark hair, and I moved my hand to stroke her head, to run my fingers through her wild mane.

She didn't speak. She didn't cry more. I didn't speak. I finally stopped petting her, and we sat still together like that for I don't know how long.

Without any indication, she stood quickly and picked up my hand, the one I had held against her head only a second before. She raised my fingers to her mouth and kissed the tip of each finger lightly. Her lips were soft and made me smile and frown at the same time. I know I moaned when she put my thumb in her mouth. When she licked and sucked, her mouth so wet and warm, I let out a low, soft moan for the duration. When she stopped, her eyes never leaving mine, she lowered my hand back to my knee. Then she left the room.

I didn't care if a maid walked in, or even her mother or my father. Right then, I relieved the pressure on my cock, making a mess of myself in my underwear. I rubbed and pulled myself, imagining her tongue, her lips, her eyes. I didn't care that it was wrong to think of her. Wrong because she was only fourteen. Wrong because she was my new stepsister. Wrong because I was twenty and only visiting for Christmas break. Wrong because my father would never allow me back if he knew. I didn't care.

I still don't.

Gillian showed more of herself to me after that first meeting. Slowly, I peeled her layers away, though always in secret. It was another year before we made love in front of this fireplace for the first time. It was a year of strange discoveries, heartbreaking and exciting discoveries.

I open my eyes again, the memories lost. The flames burn brighter with my tears.

Gillian, my love, why did you choose to run from me?

San Francisco: Simon Lamb

"This is me." I already knew this but keep it to myself. The doorman opens for us and stares at me, then Grace's ass. I let her lead the way, liking the view of her too. When the elevator doors open, a woman holding a small dog moves to the side to let us on with a polite smile. I push Grace back against the elevator wall and grab her hair to hold her for a rough kiss, loudly banging her head. I can see the woman watching us in the mirrors or trying to act like she isn't anyway. Grace doesn't give a shit; she grabs my shoulders and holds me harder against herself. When it's her floor, she shoves against me to free her mouth and loudly says, "This is us."

I let her go and follow her out, giving a small polite nod to the woman. Public displays of inappropriate behavior are a favorite hobby of mine—a cheap thrill. Grace's too, it would seem.

She already has the door open by the time I step behind her. I grab her arm so she can't move too far into the apartment, but she's on me even before I can pull her back. Her chest slams into me, hand reaching into my hair and pulling my face down to hers by my ear. I wince as her nails dig into the back of my head.

I bite her lower lip to get her to stop. She licks her tongue out, running it over my teeth instead. I let go, and so does she. I shove her against a wall, and we're both breathing hard. Our eyes rape each other. I've missed seeing her, missed having her, and she's equally hungry for me.

I step into her body, but she puts her hands on my chest to stop me. I look down at her hands, and she rips my shirt open. A button flies off. We both laugh. I yank her shirt open in return. Her small tits are high and beautiful in a red laced lattice bra. I shove this down and lick her nipples. She's sensitive, pushing into me more, gasping and moaning as I bite down. My tongue runs back up her neck to her mouth. She always tastes so sweet. Both my hands get lost in her mass of hair.

She yanks her jeans off, and I see she's without underwear again. I smile, pulling my own pants and boxers off just as fast. Her hands are on me before I can straighten back up. Her nails scrape against my chest, down the muscles of my stomach. I hiss and tense, but she stops quickly with both hands wrapped around my hard cock. I suck in a breath at her strong stroke up and down. My eyelids lower; I've pictured this, imagined being with her again.

I open my eyes. She smiles up at me, and I have a hard time keeping a straight face with her expert touch on my dick. I push both her shoulders back hard against the wall. She only smiles more. Damn, she's perfect. Before I can react or make a move, she jumps up like I'm a tree she wants to climb. Without missing a beat, I grab her ass to catch her against me, pulling her open as her legs wrap around my hips. Her hands grab onto my neck, and she leans her face into mine. "Fuck me as hard as you can, Trust. I can take it. I need you, baby." Her voice is deep and longing. Her lust matches mine. I don't give a shit if she's thought of me or not. I've pictured fucking her in every position. She's my fantasy come true.

Pushing inside her is easy; she's wet for me. I hold her against the wall and pump into her as hard as I can. Her legs and arms squeeze me tighter. She bites down on my chest. I only feel her pussy clamping down on me harder with each push in and out. I'm moaning out loud with her. When she starts to come, she knocks her head against the wall, screaming and arching into me more. I yank her hair and force her head back further, biting her neck and feeling her scream against my lips. I let my own loud cry out when I come deep inside her.

I let her body slide down mine, pulling out of her as our breathing slows. I give one last tug of her hair, one last bite to her lower lip, before pulling away completely. She stumbles a little on our pile of clothes, not picking anything up as she heads towards the bedroom.

I leave my pants and boxers on the floor too and head into the kitchen for something to drink. There's not much to choose from, just water or beer. It's early, but I grab a beer and take it with me to follow her into the bedroom.

The cleaning service must have been here recently. The place is more picked up than when I snuck in. Her clothes are more neatly piled at least. I walk around to the bathroom and find Grace touching up her makeup. She's still in only her bra and open shirt though; her ass cheeks are just visible as she leans forward. She smiles at me in the mirror, like it's the most natural thing for us to be here, almost naked, together. I put the beer down next to her and go to the toilet.

Some women are touchy about this, a guy taking a piss in front of them. Grace acts like it's nothing; she even hums to herself. I close my eyes for a second, enjoying the release and the sound of her sweet voice—low and dreamy.

"What the *fuck* is going on here?!" I didn't hear the guy come in. Apparently, Grace didn't either. It's not the boyfriend but his brother. He's glaring between Grace and me. Her look of pure shock makes me laugh, but it does suck to be in this situation sans pants and with my dick hanging limp over a toilet. I try to make the best of it and finish pissing at least.

Grace turns back around to the mirror, giving a cool and composed look to the brother. "What are you doing here, Josh?"

Josh takes one big step towards Grace and whirls her around to face him. He looks her up and down, but she stands like a perfect depiction of stony beauty, one that could only be described by Greek mythology. No mere mortal would be able to withstand her icy stare. I think about getting in between them but only continue watching her. She shows no shame, no shyness, no flinching at his obvious rage. There's no attempt to cover her nakedness. She's clearly not afraid of him, so I decide to hang back.

I don't move when he grabs her arms and shakes her. "You fucked this guy?!"

Her look remains the same, even with the bobbling of her head. He finally stops but keeps his hands on her. "You're a fucking whore!" He spits this at her.

And she laughs, with her low thick laugh, "I thought *that* was obvious!" So I was right the first time; she did fuck him too.

He pulls back and slaps her, with the back of his right hand, straight across her mouth. I watch this, still not moving. I'll put a stop to it in a minute, but for now, I want to see what she does. It's a rare opportunity to see another man hit her, to see how she reacts to such an obvious attempt to dominate her physically.

She slowly brings her face back up to his and licks her lip. No fear, no anger, no pain—it's almost her impassive look. We're both watching her closely. "That will be the last time you get to do that to me, Josh. Hope you enjoyed it."

I've had enough of this fuck touching what's mine. I flush the toilet. Josh turns to me, and Grace quickly springs out of his reach. I only smile, waiting to see if this idiot will actually make a move on me. He seems to decide that, even in my undressed state, he shouldn't try it. I'm quite a lot bigger, in height and build. He turns his head to Grace instead. "Get rid of him and come right back here."

I laugh but wait for Grace to reply, just to see how she reacts to his lame attempt again. She only shakes her head, a small smile on her face. She really is beautiful—a cat ready to pounce, a girl ready to laugh, a woman of infinite possibilities, all breathtaking.

"I think *you* should go, Josh." I say this quietly, only a little hint at a warning, an even smaller hint at a laugh. I lock eyes with Grace and smile at her as he turns his head back to me. I don't flex. I don't even tighten my hands into fists. It's best to stay relaxed and open until your opponent makes a first move.

He does, but it's only to turn to the door and throw one more look at Grace. "Then get your shit and get the fuck out of here. *Before* my brother gets home."

We stay looking at each other, her look blanking, until we hear the front door slam. She breaks the stare first, moving back in front of the mirror and looking at her face. I walk out to the front and put my pants back on but return to the bedroom quickly. Grabbing the bag from the corner, I throw her clothes inside; most everything fits. I grab a gym bag from the closet and empty the contents onto the bed, making room for the rest of her shit.

She hasn't moved from the mirror, applying a little makeup to the side of her mouth slowly. I have her clothes from the front and throw these at her when she turns to me. "Get whatever you want from here. We're leaving." I expect her to say something, put up a pretense that she's not going anywhere, but she only nods and slowly puts her things into a bag.

She's a strange girl. I can't get a read on her again. She's not showing remorse, no shame or guilt. She's not even sad, just doing it. Just doing as she's told? No. It can't be that simple. She didn't respond to the brother with any sort of submissiveness, even though it was obvious he thought she would when he tried to order her around. So she *was* submissive with him before but not now.

I chose her last year because she was so withdrawn, so sheltered. She was so broken as to be a challenge. Could I take a broken girl and break her again, remake her into what *I* wanted, not what she already was. She *was* definitely submissive then, to everyone and everything, like she didn't want her existence to leave any impression at all.

But the girl I've seen since has been the opposite. Mostly. She's been brazen and bold, confident and cold. Any hints of natural submission have been squashed. She's been a pendulum, swinging from one extreme to the next. This is a different extreme; she's resigned and completely pliant.

When she has her bag filled, she turns to me and doesn't move—like she's waiting for instructions, like she's completely at my command now. And this pisses me off. I grab her arm in a tight grip, knowing I'm leaving bruises on her arms. "Come on." She doesn't resist at all.

I grab both the bags of clothes in my free hand, not letting go of her arm, squeezing a little harder even. When we get to the front door, I stop her from opening it by yanking her back to me. She doesn't make a sound, only looks up at me with the same resigned look. "Leave your keys." She fishes them out of her purse, not even trying to get loose from my hand. She leans over to a table and puts them on it quietly.

I keep my grip on her all the way down and out the building. We don't say anything. I walk her this way the two blocks to my car. She never even tries to speak or move away, not even when I dump her bags in my trunk, not even when I shove her down into the passenger seat and slam her door, not even when I get into the car and drive her away.

I wanted today to be the start of something more between us, but this is not how I pictured it. I'd imagined making her an offer to jumpstart her modeling. I'd wanted to give her a golden carrot of some sort, entice her to come to me, get her to *want* to come to me. I'd made a plan to slowly knock down all her resistance and make her completely submissive to me, not drag her away like a whipped bitch from a pile of shit she made on the floor.

I haven't done anything to make her this submissive, and it's really starting to piss me off. I realize that I don't even know where I'm heading. I pull over and turn off the car. I don't want to take her back to my apartment, not like this. I want to dump her ass on the side of the road and keep going. She remains sitting quietly with her fucking makeup bag still on her lap, her hands still at her sides.

"Do you have somewhere to go, somewhere to stay?" I know the answer already.

"No." Her voice is flat. It's not weak, but it's not her usual sensual deep either. I turn to look at her. I know she's lying to me. Why? She has two apartments in her name. So why tell me she doesn't have anywhere to go?

"Shit." I hiss under my breath through gritted teeth and start the car again. Goddamn shit. I need a minute to think, and I can't do it sitting in my car on the street with fucking zombie girl. This is what obsession gets you! Grandfather's voice mocks me in a way he never did in real life.

Seattle: Miles Vanderson

"Yes, Ingrid. That will be all for tonight." I dismiss the servant, watching as she avoids knocking her head on the dining table as she stands.

"Good night, Mr. Vanderson." She gives a quick bow of her head before bolting out of the room.

I don't bother zipping up my pants as I also stand and retire for the night. Ingrid's ministration to my needs was efficient, perhaps not very creative or good, but hopefully it does the job to help me relax somewhat.

Closing the door on my bedroom softly, I realize my hands are fists. The muscles comprising my arms, shoulders, back are knotted and aching again. I crack my neck side to side, trying to remove the yoke of tension once more. My body has been on edge, a bundle of pent-up nervous energy. It's like I've stored up all my needs, worries, and anxieties over the last three years in every nerve ending.

It's no use though. I won't relax with the images I now have in my head.

Gillian is living with a man. *My* Gillian shacked up with some scum of the earth, new moneyed… I breathe. "It won't do any good to go down this path again, Miles." I say these words out loud, talking myself out of the heated words I feel on my tongue.

I adopt the soothing tone my mother used when I was a child. Even though I haven't talked to *her* in years, cutting off all contact after my father married Anya, I can still hear her sweet voice putting me to bed.

I cut off ties with Mother after I met Gillian. I used it as an excuse to get closer to Father, to be granted further access to his home and new family. He had no use for my mother; I needed to prove that I was *his* son more than hers. I needed to claim my rightful place as his heir, as the future of his beloved company.

He never suspected my real motivation for wanting to be closer. He was blind when it came to people. He understood dollars and stats more than feelings and behavior. Martin Vanderson was a genius in business but an imbecile at home.

And Miles Vanderson, his son and only hope for the continuation of his legacy? I am a genius in both. I smile at this thought. I know it's not completely true, only half. If I was a genius at home, I would've seen through the lies Gillian told me. I would've known she was planning her escape. I would've stopped her before she ever had a chance to step one foot out of my reach, before she ever had the chance to become this Grace Martin person she's pretending to be.

That was yet another spite to me, I'm sure, choosing a name that ties her to my father more than me. She's rubbing my nose in my failed plans for us.

Getting into bed nude, the cool sheets are comforting against my electrified skin. I lie perfectly still, my steepled fingers on my chest rising and falling the only movement, as I relive the past. I might as well; I won't be getting the rest I need tonight. I won't be able to quiet my mind. I haven't been able to silence my thoughts since Gillian entered my life six years ago.

I might as well torture myself with the memories I have. It's a familiar bedtime story I like to savor: the Prince saving the poor Stepsister from an evil witch, the white knight hero that always gets the girl in the end. Their happily ever after is always an epic love story for the ages.

Gillian did need saving. The fairytales of old never held a candle to the horrors that girl had been through. Her body was a litany of miseries at the hands of her mother. Her tears were the ink that dried all too quickly after each new grim fable. Her mind was shattered with too many tales to be held together in one volume.

Gillian was the sum of all her terror, more beautiful than any girl has the right to be after experiencing so much evil. But she wasn't untouched by that evil, not always. There were moments when I would witness the real her. I'd see the parts she kept hidden away, safe behind her vacant, unblinking, angelic face.

I'd catch a glimpse when she was doodling at the kitchen table while the staff prepared breakfast around her; when she was angry, smashing and thrashing around, thinking no one would see her; when she was seductive, using her body to tease and tempt any male around; and my personal favorite, when she was withdrawn, shelling up in herself to avoid more anguish, reading her books. She was all of these, hidden behind her innocent and pleasant facade.

I never understood how my father failed to see any of this. The staff all took notice of her odd behaviors, but they were all too well paid and trained to say anything. Her mother knew. Of course she did. She was the witch in this story.

I did see what my father saw in her mother though. Anya had played him. Or she thought she had. She had no idea the prison she was signing up for when she agreed to marry the wealthy Martin Vanderson so quickly. She was beautiful, a 31 year old version of Gillian. She was charming and sweet, at least when she was around other people. She never showed her true self to anyone except her daughter and, of course, me. My father never saw the real Anya; of that, I am sure.

Eventually, she showed herself to me. I forced her to. It was almost a year after Anya and Gillian moved into my father's house before it happened. It was almost a year after

Anya lost the baby that had tied her to her fate with my father, the baby she had originally used to tie my father to her. It was almost a year after I saw Gillian in the library that first time.

Thinking through these memories does calm me because I always get to this part of the story and can almost feel Gillian's presence with me again.

Gillian did need saving, and I *was* her white knight of sorts. I smile into the dark, relaxing my hands onto my chest with the warmth of these memories. A sigh escapes and I almost think I could sleep, if only to have Gillian in my dreams.

San Francisco: Simon Lamb

Sitting on my sofa, Grace looks smaller. She's curled into herself, unresponsive. I don't sit, still trying to think. "That wasn't your boyfriend?" I know the answers to all my questions, but I just want to get her talking again. She only shakes her head. "Look at me!" Her head snaps up in attention. "Fucking answer me, no shaking or nodding, but fucking words. Got it?!"

She starts to nod but stops. "Okay." The vacant look starts to fade. It's something anyway. "No. He was not my boyfriend." Her voice is still flat though.

"Was he always that rough with you?" I want to know this answer.

Grace only shrugs and looks away, but she quickly brings her eyes back to me when I take a step towards her. "Not always." Something shifts in her look again. A fierceness is added to her expression; her voice deepens. "Only when I *allowed* him to be. When I let him play out his little fantasies of being a man."

I smile at this. She stretches her body, coming out of her shell more. I watch her change. Her limbs relax and she leans her head to the side to look at me, twirling her hair lethargically. She's back to dancing her other hand around her tiny body too. "Did it excite you, Trust?"

I laugh and finally sit down in a chair opposite her. She's certifiably nuts. I've come to that conclusion. She must be. She bounces from one extreme to the next. Drugs? I look at her arms. No signs of any so far, but maybe she's a secret pill popper. "Are you on drugs, Red?"

"I saw how turned on you got…when Josh slapped me. I couldn't help seeing your cock get hard for me." She's doing her best seductive lounging—touching her face, teasing me with her eyes and body. But I'm not in the mood for cat and mouse.

I laugh again but add with a menacing tone, "Answer my question, or you're going to see what a real smack feels like."

She pouts and wiggles her tits playfully. "Is that all you men ever want to do with a poor defenseless girl?" I gotta give it to her; she makes me laugh. And all her lifelessness is gone at least. She's fully aware that my threat was real, but she's not afraid at all. She's asking for it, teasing and tempting.

I lean forward, elbows on my knees. "You don't want to play with me, Red. You'll lose. See, *I* won't stop with only a little smack to your face."

"Grace." I frown at her. "Call me Grace." She's sitting up, a little back from me now. Her pout is more real this time. Her face is a little softer than I've seen before.

"All right, *Grace*. Now answer me like a good girl. Are you using drugs?"

She only shakes her head. "Good." I think I believe her. So she's just nuts, the regular kind. That I can handle. That I expected. "Simon." I grin at her frowning pout. "You may call me Simon."

"Nice to meet you, *Simon*." She sarcastically stresses my name to sound sexier, hissing it at me. All softness is gone again.

"So you don't have anywhere to go? Anywhere I can take you?" I haven't leaned back, still pushing towards her. She's relaxed again, but she reaches slowly towards my hand. She's like a lioness inching towards its prey before it leaps in chase.

She shakes her head slowly with the best come-fuck-me look I've seen on her face. "Can't I stay here with you,

Simon?" Her voice got a little deeper, almost a whisper at my name. I can feel my cock twitch in response.

She *is* batshit nuts. I thought maybe she lied before because she was in shock or something. Maybe she just didn't want to be alone right then. But now? She's back to her confident, assertive attitude. So why lie? Why ask to stay with a stranger? Why act helpless?

I lean back, pulling my hand from her loose fingers. "Why do you want to stay with me, Grace?"

"Why not?" She looks around my place, nonchalant. "It's nice here. You're nice. We fuck nice. It would be nice to stay here."

I laugh at her answer. "I'm *not* nice." She only raises an eyebrow in response. "And I don't live *here*."

Her eyes narrow at this. "You *said* this was *your* place." She sounds angry, like *she'd* have reason to be angry with *me* if I lie to her?

"It is, but I don't *live* here. My home is in Alexander Valley, outside the city."

Her smile is big again. "Sounds nice. I could use a little down time."

I should kick her out. I should get rid of her craziness right now and forget all about my obsession, but that's not me. If I could forget my obsessions so easily, I wouldn't be the man I am. For now, I'm tied to her, at least until I have her screams in my head, lulling me to sleep.

I let my smile slowly spread, knowing it's both handsome and alarming. She only brightens more, smiling more herself. "All right. We can go to my house and stay there." She nods and relaxes back into the sofa, like she's won a game of chess. "But let's get a few things straight first, Red." She frowns at me again. "I meant what I said. I'm *not* nice. I won't *be* nice from here on out." She smiles again, acting as if I'm telling a joke and she already knows the ending.

She can't be so crazy that she's missing the tone I'm using, that she's missing my darkened look of warning…can she? I search her eyes and can't get past the stony smile. So she's not batshit crazy. No, just hardened. Maybe she doesn't believe me? Or maybe she thinks that I only mean the games she played with Josh or any other guy that's tried to dom her? I don't know if it's a new level of cruelty—my desire to give her forewarning. Am I now a cat that bats the mouse around, even when we both know how it will end anyway?

I'm thrown by the overwhelming urge to shock her, to see the first look of fear in her eyes. I realize that I've not seen any from her. Is that why I'm still obsessed? It's part of it, I'm sure. The closest she's been to afraid was over the fucking crayons and pancakes at the restaurant, and even that was more panic than real fear. I want to see true fear from her—fear *of* me—but I can wait. I'm patient. I've had to wait for her all this time; I can wait a little longer to get a good look at her when she's stripped of everything except fear.

I stand up, putting my hand out to her. "Coming with me now, Grace, you'll be leaving behind whatever life you have here. You won't be returning…at least, I can promise you won't return as the same woman you are now." She lowers her head, but not before I see her look blank once more. I give her all the time she needs to think.

This *is* what I wanted, to have her come to me willingly. It's a different kind of challenge, one I've had before but not quite like this, not quite like her. I've never been honest with a girl before, not before I have her in chains anyway. And my products have always been for sale—for others, trained to others' tastes. I've not truly given myself such a present before. I've used and abused, taken and trained, then tossed aside quickly every girl I've been with since Raquel. This would be different.

Train Grace to keep her? Train her to my sole desires? I smile at the challenge. I don't think the girl exists that can meet my specifications. But Grace…maybe. She's already so broken, obviously. That's a part of the challenge though, isn't it?

When she looks up at me again, her eyes are wide and almost child-like, her mouth is a little open, lips wet. She's truly exquisite. She slowly reaches with her hand to place it in mine, and I gently pull her up to me. In a faraway voice that matches her look, "Let's go."

I pull her to me a little more. I lift her chin with one finger, pushing her head back to a severe angle, like in the black and white movies my grandfather loved when the hero would smash his lips against the girl and her head would be painfully shoved into submission. "I want to be clear with you, Grace. I'm not playing a game. I'm not pretending or fantasizing. I've never been this honest with a woman before." She still looks faraway, like a soft lens has been used to soften every part of her, not unemotional but almost.

"When I say I won't be nice…it's closer to the truth to say that I will be cruel. I'm not offering you safety or love; I'm not offering you romance with tender kisses. What I offer most consider sadistic and brutal; the best of what I offer is my respect if you can be what I want, what I demand."

She slowly reaches with her other hand up to my neck, and I allow her to pull my head down towards hers. The completed picture of the movie kiss, our lips press firmly together. Before she lets go of my neck, she whispers, "Aren't all men cruel and brutal in their own way?"

I grin close to her lips, rubbing my nose against hers. "Not all are as good at it as I am, sweetheart."

I pull back to look into her eyes one more time. I was prepared to take her last year. I was ready to steal her away from her life, albeit a small life. I was ready to torture her, force her into submission. Somehow, to take her to be mine, I want her compliance; I want her willing submission right from the start. If she's to be mine, she needs to understand that this has always been her fate.

"What I don't offer you is a choice. I don't offer you a right to choose what happens to you. You've not had that choice for a while, even if you didn't know it. I only want to know that you understand that we leave here now, together…and you have chosen this by your every action, by your very being, Grace, since I first noticed you. Do you understand that?"

She nods, still with the faraway, dreamy smile on her face. "I've never had choices. I wouldn't know what they look like." She pats my cheek gently, her voice becoming even more airy, eerie, "And I know you don't have any choice either, Simon. You are who you are, and we will be what we will be. Maybe we will have what we need finally…in the end."

I let go of her hand and grab her arm hard like before, in the same spot so I know it will hurt her—a taste of what's to come. Her dreamlike face doesn't change though, not even when I yank her out of this apartment and out of this life.

Seattle: Miles Vanderson

I knew Gillian wasn't a normal teenager when I met her that first winter. She wasn't the usual girl with friends and interests when I saw her on my frequent visits after that either. She was always hiding behind her straight-faced, smooth exterior around people, always being exactly the perfect child that was expected of her.

Gillian became more with me. In time, I was able to crack through the ice she showed to others. Or rather, I was able to get inside those cracks. I smile in the dark with this thought. Yes, that's more accurate. Gillian had many cracks in her mind, and I got through them all eventually. I cracked her wide open and made her mine.

Gillian was always affectionate with me, like she was that first time. It was always in secret though. She'd find ways to touch me, entice me. She'd rub her hand down my back as she'd come down the stairs to stand in attendance at the door at the beginning of a party. She'd put her finger in my mouth as she'd lean over to say good night. She'd lift her skirt to reveal just the hint of her underwear when we were alone. She would dance in front of the fire so I could see her body through her thin clothing. All in secret, it became our game.

I found more reasons to be at home, just to be near her so I could play our wicked games. I no longer waited for her to do something. I would tell her what to do, and she did it. I became bolder, more demanding, as the months wore on, and she did exactly as I told her to do. It was my first taste of the power that I would come to crave.

I didn't touch her, not exactly, only indulging over her clothes. I would make her stay perfectly still while I touched her in the gentlest ways. I'd graze her stomach, her new breasts, her back, her legs, and once, between her legs, under her skirt but over her underwear. I made her put that pair of pink panties under my pillow, all in secret.

I stayed away for months after that. I kept the underwear hidden inside a pair of socks in the back of my drawer, but I kept away from her. I tried to stay away as well, but I was weak with longing for her.

I know it isn't the usual fairytale story of romance, but Gillian *did* need my love. She needed me there. She needed a protector.

I saw what her mother did to her. Gillian never broke her silence, not even when I saw it with my own eyes. She never admitted the bruises and welts were Anya's doing. Gillian was very good at keeping secrets by then. That first year of getting to know each other, I would only gently touch a bruise or other angry mark, and she would just smile, letting me.

It wasn't until the next Christmas, when I couldn't stay away any longer, that things changed.

Father and Anya had been away on business trips for weeks before. It took all of my restraint to stay away while I knew Gillian was home alone. I knew our games were heading down a path that I couldn't stop though. All I could do was stay away.

I'd surprised the household staff by arriving earlier than expected for that second Christmas break. I was excited to see Gillian again. I wanted to show her the present I'd brought for her. I was determined to make up for our lost time. I was going to start fresh with her.

I'd reasoned with myself that when she was older, we could have a real relationship; I just needed to wait for her. I loved her. I would've waited a million blue moons for her if it meant we could truly be together, that our love wouldn't need to be a secret forever. I was a fool in love.

I asked the cook where Mrs. Vanderson was, and I was told she thought Anya had gone out for a drive since the sun had melted the ice off the roads for the first time in days. I knew Father was still at the office and wasn't expected for hours. It was my chance to see Gillian alone before the holiday parties and family gatherings.

I raced up to her room, not bothering to knock when I heard her muffled voice inside. She was the only one who knew I was arriving that day, and I had told her I wanted to see her right away. She knew I had news to share with her.

The scene I walked in on is one that has haunted me even to this day. It changed the course of our lives. Even now I shudder with the memory of it. It was the first time I saw Gillian fully nude.

And Anya had clearly just beaten her, my beautiful naked Gillian. There was a belt in Anya's hand still, raised and ready to be lowered again. Gillian was on her knees before her mother. Anya was sitting on the bed with her legs spread.

The looks on their faces are perpetually frozen in my mind. Perhaps, because they were both still for so long, each not moving from their spots in the room. The belt sagged, but Anya's arm remained raised. I, too, stood frozen in the doorway.

My memory tricks me. It's a dreadful game I play with myself because I know we each moved, and quickly at that, but I remember the details as though we were locked in place, made statuesque by the moment we were caught in.

Gillian's face rises like a ghost before my eyes now. She had two tear-stained streaks running down her white cheeks, but her eyes were free of any tears. Her gaze held its usual unreadable darkness as she turned her head towards me. The icy stare she hid behind didn't change. Her long dark hair was trained into a thick braid so all of her body was laid bare. I could see the belt marks that crossed almost every inch of her back, butt and stomach. She was already black and blue in places, but Anya had taken care not to hit her anywhere that would be seen once she was clothed again. She always did.

Anya's face was the opposite. Her eyes were electric with rage and insanity. Her cheeks flushed with it. Her chest rose and fell quickly. Her underwear was abandoned on the floor next to Gillian; her dress was pulled up high to her waist. I could see her excitement. Her voice broke the spell.

I open my eyes, seeing only my darkened bedroom again. The flashbulb images of years ago are still making my heart race though. I've given up trying to understand what happened next. I've given up trying to seek forgiveness. It happened as it was going to happen. Fate or karma, I was doomed the moment I opened that door, the moment Anya spoke my name and told me to close the door behind me.

I was doomed, after all, the moment I stepped into the library the year before that and saw a young girl crying from the abuse her mother did in secret.

Anderson Valley: Simon Lamb

I always love this drive. It's fast and winding, through fields and hills, past towns built by one thing—grapes. The vines are heavy. Shiny strips of ribbon flutter on the air above darkening fruit. The scent of roses replaces the stench of the city. Warm sunshine replaces dense fog. Earth and sky replace concrete and people. It's not a long drive, but it's worlds away. And I always feel cleaner being here.

Grace has been quiet, just staring out the window as the miles pass. She hasn't moved; I was able to forget she was in the car with me. I'm glad that I chose not to toss her in the trunk. I thought about it. It's how I usually bring a girl here. It's how I usually take a girl from here.

But then, the girls aren't meant for me, so it's best if they don't know where they're going, where they've been. Grace is unique. I don't mind her seeing her destination.

I smile more as I pull into the long drive leading up to the house. It's an impressive property. Surrounded by fields of grapes, orchards of olive trees, and a network of underground caves for storing everything, the house is a solid stone structure—massive in size and stature, set up on the highest point.

In Great-Grandfather's day, this was an active vineyard. Now I only use it as my private home. Private being the key word. I have staff, but no one stays on this property. My staff are all loyal; the same family has served mine for generations. They never question my orders, my peculiar demands, and no one steps foot in the caves unless invited. Or brought.

"What do you think of your new home, Red?" Grace is still walking around the grand hall. Calling it a living room would do nothing to describe its size and lofty ceilings, or the massive furnishings and expensive antiques that have manned the same positions on the floor plan for generations. All have been passed down from Lamb to Lamb. The rug alone is worth more than most homes, and it's certainly bigger than the apartment I took her from.

She turns to me, standing in the center of the room, arms crossed. "Stop calling me that." Her voice is raised slightly, like there should be a stamping of her foot to go along with it. It's the first she's spoken since we left the city.

Smiling, I cross the room to her and slam her down to the rug with a wide swing from the palm of my right hand to her cheek. I'm impressed that there is only the slightest shriek from her as her hip and hands hit the floor. Standing over her, I'm still smiling. "Rule number 1: don't raise your voice to me, Red. Got it?"

Grace doesn't look up. She turns away from me and braces herself to stand. I let her. To my surprise, even with my obvious handprint covering half her face, she doesn't say or do anything. I know it has to hurt, but she doesn't touch her face or show any sign of tears. Instead, her face is soft and open, but she doesn't look at me.

I step towards her, expecting her to move away, but she stays perfectly still. "Look at me." She looks up obediently. I'm stiff looking into her dark eyes. There's no sign of pain. Or fear. I'm oddly even more aroused by this. Usually I only get this hard after seeing a girl brought to tears by a justly deserved shot to the mouth. But Grace is definitely not most girls.

She speaks up, almost sweet with her faraway voice, a fog circling her words, "I like to be called Grace. It's the name...the name I'd like you to use."

I put my hand gently over the red side of her face. She still doesn't flinch or move, just keeps her eyes locked to mine. "All right. When you're a good girl, I'll call you Grace."

And her look melts to her usual one of seduction—her eyes closing slightly, darkening alluringly more. She puts her hand over mine, only pressing slightly with her cool touch. "I believe we have an understanding then, Simon." It's about the sexiest thing I've heard in a long time.

It brings me back to the first time I hit Raquel. I'd always known that my sexual desires drifted to the more sadistic, darker side. I was the kid who got in trouble for spanking the teacher's ass or holding down a girl and pinching her non-existent tits on the playground. I learned by the time I was seven that I had to indulge my tendencies in private only.

Grandfather paid off and sent away more than one maid after I'd coerced them into spreading their knees and submitting to my painful touches. His solution was to send me to all-boys schools and only have male help around the house. It only fueled my urges and fantasies, and one particularly helpful driver introduced me to darker erotica at an early age. He showed me a world in books where my desires were met.

Meeting Raquel was the start of all things good for me. She wasn't willing, not at first. She laughed off the invitation I gave her to come over for a swim. I'd met her at one of Grandfather's boring society dinners. She blushed and flirted with me all night but tried to act like I was a child.

The shrink Grandfather hired after her suicide tried to make it seem like I was a child too—that she took advantage of me. I had his eyes popping with the details of my repeated sexual depravity with her. I left no doubt who was in control each and every time.

He then tried to say that it was my way of acting out from early childhood abandonment issues. As if never knowing my mother and losing my father just as I was old enough to remember him were reasons for my carnal lusts. As if I fucking gave any thought to either of my parents while I whipped and tortured the girl.

No, my desires, my needs were always the same for as long as I can recall. I've not really stopped to analyze them. The trips to the shrink were to appease Grandfather, no more. I knew what I wanted with Raquel and with every girl since her—sex. Rough. Sadistic. Sex. The need to cause pain during pleasure, the need to hear screams as much as moans, the need to see my sadistic touch on smooth flesh—it's all I've ever wanted. Raquel was just the first to give in to my needs.

I wasn't surprised when Raquel showed up at the exact time I told her to. Even then, I understood the nuance of picking the right girl. I understood that there are willing victims in this world, girls that will give themselves over to the cruelest of desires, their own needs matched by them. Sometimes, I have to help them to see their needs for what they truly are. Sometimes, I have to introduce them to these needs. But there is always a moment when I know that I have the girl right where I want her, a moment when she'll submit to anything I demand.

With hardly a command, Raquel had stripped out of her clothes to reveal a tiny bikini, laughing and smiling at me as she plunged into our indoor pool. I watched her splash around a little before calling her over to me at the steps. I will never forget her look that first time I smacked her, that first moment when I knew I had her. The first look on the first girl I knew for the first time was all mine to do with as I pleased....it's a memory I cherish.

Raquel was perfect—hair wet and stuck to her shoulders, arms flailing at the water, face red from the slight slap, eyes wide with shock and pain. She had the most beautiful look to her eyes. There was fear, sure, but understanding too.

When I told her to take off my shorts and suck me, I can admit, now anyway, that I wasn't sure she would obey. There was the smallest hesitation before her fingers sought the top of my swimsuit, but I knew after that. I knew the look in her eyes. I saw it many times after that, from her and others.

Before she left that day, I said something like what Grace just said to me about an understanding. And I still get hard thinking about that first girl's response, "Yes, Sir."

Grace has the same look in her eyes now. She understands what we both need. Something else lingers in her darkness, though, something untouched by me. I move my hand from her cheek to her hair, grabbing a fistful of her silky curls. She drops her hand to my chest.

I like the weight of her hair. There's so much of it, so much to her. Waif as she is, angled and thin, she takes over a space.

Pulling her head back roughly, running my tongue along the now painful arch of her neck, her eyes never leave mine. "You like it rough, don't you, Grace?"

"Are you being rough?" I laugh at her bravado. I can see her breathing is quickened. Scraping my teeth against her smooth skin, across the ridge of her collarbone, I hear her little gasp escape. Her scent strengthens as I bend down to kiss the very tops of her breasts, filling my lungs with her spicy sweetness.

I bring my head back up to look down on her. "No, not yet. Be a good girl and tonight you'll sleep in my bed."

Her lips curl into a small smile. "What's my reward if I'm bad?"

Without letting her hair go, I shove her down to her knees. "You still think we're playing a game, Red. I'm going to have to disillusion you of that thought. You'll learn tonight that you have only one option." I slap her face to punctuate the next words, "Be my good girl."

Surprisingly, she doesn't raise her hands to try to stop me. She doesn't even close her eyes. She just watches as each word becomes a sting to her cheek. Slowly, she smiles, a small laugh in her voice, "My safeword is fish, Trust, not that I've ever used it."

I laugh too, shaking my head. I let her hair go, and she stands smoothly. "I know that you think this is all normal, that you're here for your own desires, by your own design, Grace. I'd even agree with that to a point. But safewords and proper bondage etiquette? The usual dance between likeminded partners, exploring the darker side of sex—that sort of shit, you can forget about."

I take her arm but do it gently, like a prince escorting his lady, steadying her gait. She doesn't need my assistance; I just want to feel her close. I walk us towards the curtained opening that leads to the dining room. A fire is still going next to the long table set for two. I'd dismissed all the staff to the adjacent property for the evening, but my dinner is still ready and waiting as ordered.

I pull a chair for Grace to sit and unfold the napkin to drape across her lap. I remove the silver dome from the plate in front of her. She smiles and thanks me. We're just a normal couple having a quiet early dinner at home. Well, it's normal for me anyway.

I take my seat and am happy to see that Grace doesn't grab her silverware like a starved hillbilly at the county fair. Despite her display of uncouth eating habits at the diner, her table manners tonight are impeccable. We eat in relative silence. There's the usual politeness of words exchanged over a well-prepared meal. Likes and dislikes are discussed but only about food and wine.

"You live here alone?" She appears thoughtful, looking up at the large artwork on my walls.

"Yes. Just me." I pour some more wine for us and tip my glass to her. She smiles and does likewise. "My cousins come here from time to time. Cary and Sophia are the closest thing to family I have anymore, but there's no one else. I don't like visitors." I don't like sharing information about myself either, but it seems natural to do so sitting with her in my home.

"But you brought *me* here."

"Ah, but you're not a visitor." She smiles at this, so I feel the need to clarify. "I mean that a visitor has the right to come and go, to enjoy the premises as they see fit, within social confines of course. *You* are *not* a visitor. You *can't* come and go, and you're only allowed access to what *I* give you, Grace." I smile a little more mischievously, leaning into her. "And the only enjoyment you'll have will be in pleasing me."

I begin to doubt that she understands what I said because her look doesn't change. No alarms go off in her head. She takes a tiny sip of wine and licks her lips nicely. When she responds to me, her voice is still husky and warm. "So you mean to keep me here? Against my will? Is that it? To what purpose?"

My smile is genuine, beaming at her. I was afraid for a moment that she was absolutely stupid. Crazy I can take. Stupid I can't. I fucking hate spelling everything out. "Yes. I mean to keep you here. I've meant to keep you here for some time now." She frowns slightly at this. As far as she knows, we're almost strangers. I'll keep her in the dark a little longer, reveal my knowledge of her in small increments. I want to get out of her all that I don't know already over time. "I'll let you in on a little secret, Grace."

I push back from the table, taking her hand. She rises with me, and I lead her through the grand hall again, towards the large curved stairs. I explain a few things along the way to my bedroom. "I have a job of sorts. It's one that I've given to myself—a hobby, a sport that others appreciate as well. It's lucrative, but that's certainly not why I do it. I bring women here and train them to be perfect submissives for various clients." She continues to smile, her hand relaxed against my arm.

In front of my bedroom door, she puts her hand on my chest to pause me. Leaning in with her lower body pressed to me, her eyes are nearly black under her lashes. "You mean to sell me." It's not a question. It's almost a challenge. There's no tremble to her deep voice.

I pull her face towards mine with a finger under her chin and kiss her gently. "No. I mean to keep *you* for myself." I push open the heavy wooden door, the detailed carving a testament to an artisan long since gone. It was a trophy from a trip to India from a grandfather too far removed to remember how many greats to add. She walks into my room without any hesitation, smiling at the luxury and comfort within.

I watch as she moves about, running her hand over the silks, brocades, velvets. It's an opulent room of riches, warm even on the coldest of days from the heaviness of the fabric used everywhere. The walls have been thickened too; I've made sure no sound can escape from here.

I allow the door to close loudly behind me, but she doesn't jump. She does turn, though, to stand facing me in the center of the room. Without a word, she slowly removes her clothes, letting them fall to the floor at her feet. When completely naked, she puts her hands on her hips, jutting out their boniness for me to admire, pushing her small tits back but still up. It's a runway pose that puts all her beauty on full display.

I admire her lack of fear, her boldness. For now anyway, it's refreshing. I'm used to dealing with a sniveling, begging girl at this point. Grace is full of surprises. She's kept me on my toes since I first saw her.

It's dawning on me now just how much Grace might be used to rougher play already, that she's not like the girls that have never tasted anything but vanilla for a sexual flavor.

Undoing all that's been done to her before, undoing her mindset of what she should or shouldn't do, may take a bit more finessing with her added experience. Nothing pisses me off more than a submissive trying to top from the bottom.

"Come here." She moves towards me with her cat walk. I'm only sorry that we aren't farther apart; I had only a moment to bounce my eyes between her legs and breasts. Her skin is a dewy softness in the subdued lighting. "Undress me."

She doesn't hesitate, running her tongue up the opening along my neck to my ear as her fingers work down the buttons of my shirt. She pulls gently at the belt and pants opening, questioning with her eyes about the belt. I lift my smile in response and shake my head. No, I won't be using a belt on her. I can't tell if she pouts at this news; her lips go to my chest to hide her reaction too quickly.

I've been with pre-trained submissives before. I've checked out a few clubs with Cary in the area, always with mixed feelings. Although I can appreciate an already eager and primed product, I usually find that the training is too sloppy, haphazard. The girl believes she still has some control. Well, to be fair, in those clubs, that's true. Rules of conduct all apply in those organizations, even in their so called 'no limits' rooms.

It's why I started my business—supply meeting demand—to deliver a trained product to the exact specifications of my friends and associates. My girls have no delusions of any control. I'm quite proud, boastful even in the right circles, of the fact that I've never had a product try to run after a certain level of my training. The girls all succumb to their innately submissive natures. My training brings out the very best in them. The girls understand and embrace their destinies…in time anyway.

I'm not evil, well, sort of in the eyes of those too prudish to admit the truth. Our culture is too quick to forget its past. In less than three generations ago, the women running around trying to rule the world today would have legally been treated as no more than chattel. I choose to ignore the convention of today's mores and laws. I adhere to a time long gone. It's almost nostalgic really—a romance between a Master and his property in a time forgotten. I smile at my own musings as I let Grace continue her tongue's journey down my body.

All my girls resign themselves to their fate quickly, not easily for some, but always quickly. Even for the most vanilla of my products, they learn to welcome any attention, cruel or tender, and yield to their own need to be dominated and used for pleasure. The girl does receive pleasure too. I'm not a monster. When she's good and trained, she learns that it can come in the form of whips and chains, not hearts and flowers.

It's a simple matter of selection. I take my time watching and learning about a girl before deciding that she'll be right for a particular client's needs. I suppose I knew all along that Grace would be for me. I wanted her for myself from the beginning, even as I toyed with the idea of selling her.

Grace is already on her knees, happily putting her mouth to good use. Her tongue trails up, down, and all around my stiff dick. While her lips press and squeeze, her fingers expertly rub up and down my length, pulling slightly on my balls. I could lose myself easily in the feeling, but tonight is about something much more interesting to me.

I grab a fistful of her glorious hair again, shoving her face deep against me. She's a remarkable girl, able to take all of me without any gagging. She even drops her hands to her sides, offering her mouth completely, staying relaxed. She's well-trained, but this only makes me scrutinize her more. Yanking her face away from me, her mouth stays wide open. I hold her in place, bending her back further. Her arms remain at her sides. Her tongue whips out to lick her lips; her chin is wet with moisture. Her eyes are trained on mine, but seductive, not afraid.

"You do that very well." Her lips only curl in the slightest smile. "But you didn't have my permission." I run my free hand down her cheek, bending to take one nipple between my fingers. I twist it painfully, and her eyes only close for a second, her face remaining still. She doesn't react with more than a small sigh when I squeeze harder. Interesting. Her nipples were sensitive to every touch earlier. Now, she's ice.

"You didn't have my permission to undress either." She turns her pretty lips into a pretty pout and starts to speak, still with hardly any reaction to the obvious pain I'm causing her. A slight increase in breathing, a small flush to her cheeks—that's all I get.

"And you don't have permission to speak." She's quick to pop her mouth closed, same wicked grin playing across her lips. "Face down, on the floor." I release her hair gently. She moves to the floor, a panther stretching out, not slowly, but her muscles move like oil under her skin, flexing and relaxing. Her ass is last to lower—two perfectly taut spheres with smooth, creamy skin. I have to stop a laugh at the thought of bouncing a quarter off her. Maybe later.

"You've obviously had a certain level of training before, Grace." She only nods against the rug. "I hope for your sake, sweetheart, that it doesn't interfere with my plans for you." I walk over to a large burled armoire, an antique piece that has stood in this room since the house was built. Like so much of what is here, I have conformed it to my own tastes. Inside the double doors are my favorite toys, my tools of the trade—whips, chains, cuffs, crops, canes, plugs, ropes—all neatly organized and waiting for me.

I select a short leather whip, one of my favorites. I've had to replace it several times from overuse but always come back to the precision of this style. The size is perfect for my room, almost for any room in this house, and the leather is supple in my hand. I'm not sure the girls have always appreciated the quality of the leather, but I certainly have.

The single shortened tail can still produce a good sound, but it's the closeness that I like. I can be near enough to smell the fear and pain. I can still get a good range of motion, a strong crack on flesh, but without the need to be further away like the whips I use in the cave.

Grace is beautiful on the floor, arms stretched over her head, relaxed against the rug. Her hair covers her face, fanning over her back. All of her is toned but delicate, strong but yielding. Normally, I would have the girl shackled for a first whipping, but I'm too tempted to see how Grace reacts on her own.

I push her hair to the side with the whip. Grace wiggles at the feather touch but remains silent. She knows what's coming but doesn't tense at all, only relaxes more. I raise the whip, an extension of my arm. It's a motion that is second nature to me. The whoosh is small but adds an electrifying sound to the air as the leather comes down across her back. One thin river of red appears in an oasis of creamy skin. Only one small gasp escapes from Grace.

Without delays, I bring the whip up and down many more times. A multi-lined V forms on her back—lines that stretch onto her perfect ass, up her shoulders. Still only small cries, gasps, are all I get for my artistry. Her ass rises, back arches, muscles tense for only a moment, before she quickly relaxes back into place for the next strike. She's a perfect whipping doll.

"Roll over." She turns her body, sinewy, a snake on my rug now, until she's lying exactly the same—relaxed, arms raised, legs straight in front of me. Remarkably, there's not a single tear on her cheeks, not a shadow of fear in her eyes. She smiles serenely at me even.

I smile back, narrowing my eyes and studying her for a moment. Her breathing is quick but already slowing. I know the rug has to be adding to the sting on her back, but she shows no signs of discomfort. I move the whip, and her eyes follow it but still with no look of fear to them. Perhaps she's never been whipped on her front? Maybe she has no idea of the level of pain that can be brought in this position?

"Keep very still for this, Grace." She nods. "I wouldn't want to damage your pretty face." She smiles more at this. "Have you been whipped like this before?" She nods again. Hmm.

I bring the whip up dramatically, wanting to make the first strike the hardest. Her only reaction is to close her eyes just as the whip lands across her stomach and breast. Her small cry is lost against her upper arm. Her hands clasp and clench, her knees bend only slightly, but she remains still otherwise.

With each successive whoosh and crack, her cries get a little longer, a little louder, until a moan stretches from her lips. It's intoxicating to hear her, to watch her. I feel light and almost dizzy when I'm finished. I've held my breath, not wanting to miss the slightest sound from her. Her sweet spicy scent fills the room. Not once did she cry out loudly or beg me to stop. She never showed fear, never smelled like fear, only arousal and yearning. Her legs rubbed together after the first welt.

I'm breathing as hard as she is. My blood pumps to my cock as I drop the whip. Her front is a crisscross of lines. I licked the whip down her legs, across her stomach, concentrated on her tits. She's a mess of red and cream, deeper welts begging to be kissed. "Get up. On the bed." I watch her move slowly—a cross between the snake and cat, sinewy and springy.

Her eyes are bright, but there's still only a trace of tears on her face. She wobbles a little but stands confident. Before she can move to the bed, I grab her arms and smash her against me. I have to taste her mouth; I have to feel her skin. Her tongue fights against mine, forcing its way as much as mine does, not yielding, not submissive. She's hungry and needing. Her skin almost burns mine, our sweat mingling.

I pull away but keep her close. Her eyes are fevered, her breath is panting; so is mine. I want her so much. I've never felt this before. Confusion and lust. I am usually so in control. Her show of strength against the pain, her will bent to perfect submission for each blow—it's more than I expected. It's what I've wanted from her.

I've had lesser women pass out on me after only a few stripes. Their own fear and emotions escalate the pain from every touch to an unbearable level, causing them to hyperventilate and lose consciousness before I get to anything fun. But no girl has ever taken so much so quickly, and with only the slightest hint at her level of pain.

I whisper against her, "Don't you feel anything?" I feel her cheek rise in a smile as she presses herself against me more, not to ease the pain but to embrace it. Her skin is on fire; our sweat has to be increasing the sting of the deeper welts. She glides our bodies together, gasping.

"I feel everything. You are very skilled, Simon."

I yank her away. Is she fucking with me? Playing her little game of bravado? No, her smile is serene. Her look is unmistakably one of lust and need.

Seattle: Miles Vanderson

I did close Gillian's bedroom door, quietly. I like to think that I was numb or in shock from what I was witnessing, that is why I remained still and quiet and just did as Anya said, but I don't really give myself that excuse. I have from time to time but not anymore. I've given up the uselessness of remorse. There's no one around to point an accusing finger at me anyway, and I can't blame myself. I never really did.

I closed the door because I didn't want anyone to catch us. I already had that thought in my head. *Us*. I'd been keeping secrets with Gillian for a year. This was just another secret I would share with her.

I'm alone here in my bedroom, five years since that moment. I've relived it many times, yearning for Gillian to be here with me. I've relived many memories of *us*, but I always go back to that first one. It's my usual bedtime story.

It's like a wound that I won't let heal. I feel my lips rise in a smile in the dark. No. It's not a wound. That's not fair. I relive that day because it was the real start, not the library, not the previous year of self-torture, trying to get closer to Gillian while keeping a distance. No. That day, in her bedroom, that was the start for us.

I had intended to explain my plan to her that day. I had words in my head that would explain how we could be together when she was allowed to attend college in only three short years. I had a plan for slowly getting her away from her mother; a plan to convince my father to grant me greater control of one of his smaller businesses, perhaps to set me up to buy my own, something that would allow me independence from him; a plan to marry Gillian as one last secret; a plan to make her mother of my child as quickly as possible. I knew the last would ensure Martin Vanderson would never go against our marriage, not once he knew his empire was safe, that I had provided him with what he never could: more heirs, a stronghold on his legacy.

It was a long plan, one I had thought through, or so I thought.

When I closed that door, I knew all my planning was useless. I'd seen through Anya, and she would never let me have Gillian for myself.

So I closed the door and did what I had to do to keep Gillian. I closed the door so no one would see her as she was. I closed the door for the same reason I never said anything about the abuse I knew she suffered. I can't hide from that truth, not to myself anyway. I kept Gillian's secret because it was the only way to keep her close to me.

Anya hurt her, but Gillian shared it with me. She allowed me to see her pain. She never said a word, but she allowed me to touch her. She'd put my hand where she was hurt.

I close my eyes again, seeing Gillian as the light was fading from the windows that day. It was a cool winter light that cast a soft glow over the madness in that room. I give in to the call of that memory. I let it take full control of me like it always does.

"Come closer, Miles." Anya's voice is airy like Gillian's gets sometimes.

I move closer, but I stop inches next to Gillian's bare feet and notice that they are clean. I notice her toes are pointed. What odd things to notice in the midst of all her other details.

Anya moves but not in the way I thought she would. She doesn't stand; she doesn't move to cover herself. She moves her hand to rest between her open legs, her fingers toying with the hair there. I look down and feel surreal in

*noting that Gillian has the start of soft hair between her legs
as well. Gillian's expressionless eyes continue to stare up at
me from her kneeling position. I watch her blink in silence.*

*Anya pulls my eyes to her again with her voice, "I
know you love her. She's told me." I glance quickly back to
Gillian, feeling a stab of disappointment at her betrayal, a
spike of anger at her unresponsive stare. "I could destroy
you as much as you could destroy me, Miles, but I don't
think that's what you want, is it?" I bring my eyes back to
Anya and watch, fascinated, as she puts one, two, three
fingers into herself. She moans with her eyes half-closed for
a moment before regaining composure, fingers still inserted.*

*"No. That's not what you want." I nod at her assertion,
unable to speak. "I could be pregnant even now with your
father's precious child, and you'd be ruined. Martin would
never let the truth get out, even if I'm not. It would destroy
him. He'd protect me even as he'd despise me, but you'd be
forever thrown into the icy lake of eternal damnation, Miles.
He'd never forgive you for your part in his destruction. He'd
always keep you at arms-length, and you'd never have what
you really want."*

*I know her words are true. I'd said them to myself
many nights over the last year while I tried to convince
myself to stay away. My father would never completely
disown me, not as long as I'm his sole heir; but he'd never
allow me back into his house either. He would keep me away
from Gillian.*

*"Touch her hair, Miles." The simple command brings
me out of my thoughts. I look from Anya to Gillian's head
twice. Gillian stays completely still. I marvel at her stoic
nature against the pain from the screaming bruises and*

welts her mother just inflicted. I can see new marks layered over older ones as I look closely at her.

Gillian's head is turned away from me, only looking down, not moving. Her breathing is even and slow. I reach my hand out and push my fingers into her hair. Her head is warm and her hair is soft, like always.

Gillian's changed since I last saw her though. The softness of a child is gone. Her dark beauty is even more pronounced with her sharp angles and lean body.

Anya smiles up at me, and I watch her fingers move in and out of herself. I move my fingers on Gillian's head in the same slow rhythm, lulled and hypnotized. "Your father is old; his health is starting to go. He can't live forever, Miles. And when he's gone, I'll let you have Gillian all to yourself." She releases the belt she's still holding and holds out her free hand to me. I keep my hand on Gillian's head and grasp Anya's outstretched fingers with my other.

And so we were joined that day, the three of us. Joined in secrecy, it was a fresh start of sorts.

I'd closed the door and sealed our fates.

Anderson Valley: Simon Lamb

Walking Grace backwards, keeping her upper body tight against mine, keeping our lips searching each other, we reach the edge of my bed. I trail my tongue along her salty skin, up and down the curve of her neck, breathing in the heat from her hair as I pull her earlobe into my mouth, nibbling the edge. She's hungry for me, rubbing her lower lip against the stubble of my cheek, reaching with her tongue to taste me.

She hasn't closed her eyes, not completely, and the lust hasn't left them either. I let go of one arm and run my hand down her back, feeling the marks that are raised and deep. Her gasps aren't of pain at my touch, more moans of want. She arches into my hand, pressing herself to my fingers, begging with her body for more. I oblige her, pinching my way down the length of one stripe to its end at her luscious ass, finding another to pinch harder. Her moan doesn't stop, but her teeth sink into my chest.

"Fuck." I grab a fistful of hair and yank her head away from me. Her smile is fleeting but obviously a challenge as she licks her lips. "I'm not into pain, Red, only giving it."

"How do you know unless you try it, Trust?" Her voice is syrupy sweet and dripping with lust. "I could show you." Her eyebrow raises seductively with her lips.

I pull her hair harder, hoping to see her eyes glass with pain instead of just the lust I still see. Her lips at least lose their smirk. "I'm the teacher, Red. You're the student. Apparently, you haven't learned your lesson yet." I pull her hair harder still, enough to lower her to the bed. Her back arches and legs bend to ease the stress on her head, but damn her eyes and face! Only lust. No fear. No pain. Her body responds, but only in its own want. She bends to me, but only in her own need.

I stare between her eyes, lost for a moment in my frustration. I let her go, dropping her upper body onto the bed. She remains half on, half off, her face still and calm. She waits patiently for me to make the next move. And I stand above her like an animal in heat, panting and looking over her naked and inflamed body. I can't decide what to make of her willful denial of the pain and fear I've inflicted on her.

Her lack of usual response, what I expect from a girl put in this situation, is unnerving me. Fuck! I close my eyes and take one more second to get control of my emotions. I'm never at a loss when it comes to a woman naked and in my bed. I'm not about to let Grace get the better of me on her first night here. I won't let her see how she's mystified me. I won't give in to the chaos she's creating in my mind and body.

Opening my eyes slowly, I take in her beauty. I allow the marks I've left on her to have their full effect on me. I feel my cock throb and grin in response to her serene stare. Her expression isn't giving me what I want, but her body certainly is.

Seattle: Miles Vanderson

Fate. Karma. Gillian said it was our stars. I laughed at her whenever she spoke about her belief in astrology.

It was one of her quirks. She'd sit quietly during the day, withdrawn and concentrating, writing and researching through her charts and books. Then she'd read our horoscopes from that day to each of us before going to bed. She always wanted to know if they were accurate, if our days had played out the way the stars had told her to write them. It was odd that she usually gave us our horoscopes for the day that had already been, not the future that could still be, but it was a part of her quirk.

Father indulged her little hobby. He'd ask her for a prediction about one of his business dealings, and she'd very seriously answer him. He never laughed at her.

Anya was less indulgent of course, but she remained quiet since Father seemed amused by it. She'd laugh along with me, acting as if her daughter was a great joy to her. I knew the truth.

Neither of us laughed that night though. Gillian read her daily predictions as usual, but she only asked Father for an accuracy rating. She already knew that her stars had spoken the truth for the rest of us.

I don't remember the specifics of her predictions that night. I only remember the feeling they created in me as she read them aloud. I kept glancing at Father, hoping that he wouldn't get suspicious of their not so hidden meaning. Gillian was all but spelling out the events of that day, a confession through astrological charting, planetary alignments and conjunctions.

Anya and I remained silent, not looking at each other at all. Gillian went to bed early that night. I stayed awake long after the rest of the house went dark and quiet.

It was the start of my almost nightly ritual of reliving the events of that day over again. I sat in the library with a forgotten and unfinished glass of something in my hand, the fire burning my unblinking eyes, and I relived the scene from earlier in Gillian's bedroom.

I've thought so often of that day that I could retrace every step, remember every touch down to the finest of details without leaving anything out. At will, I can picture Gillian's eyes and how they never lost their vacant stare, not even when Anya picked up the belt again. I can recall how she didn't cry out even when Anya hit her twice on the same darkened spot, how she didn't speak, didn't beg or plead. Gillian's tears never came, not even when I pushed Anya onto the bed to be readily accepted between her open legs.

Gillian stayed on her knees, motionless, watching us. Ours was a fast, sweaty, nearly silent copulation. But we both stared at Gillian as we came, pressed together on her bed.

I left the room quickly after in a fog. Anya's voice followed me to the door, echoing the words in my own head.

"We are one now, Miles. You, me, Gillian. We are joined together now and forever."

She repeated something similar to me often over that next year. That we were joined, bonded, a true family not to be broken. Only her death tore us apart.

I sigh again in my lonely, dark bedroom, eyes open and unseeing. I didn't question the validity of what Anya said because I didn't care. I was reckless with love and lost with lust from that day on. I dove into the mess of our relationship, *us*, we three intertwined, from then on.

I only cared about keeping Gillian close to me. I did what I had to do, and I kept Gillian safe. I did.

I close my eyes again to continue with my bedtime story, to see Gillian's face once more.

Anderson Valley: Simon Lamb

I put my knee on the bed in between Grace's open legs. She's wet and hot against me, grinding into me as I push her further onto the bed. Her hands reach for me and I grab her wrists, forcing her arms down as I position myself above her, straddling her left leg.

Her smile up at me twists a little. I can almost see her mind working. In this position, I'm vulnerable. "Try it and see what it gets you, Red." And I almost mean it. I almost want her to fight me. I almost want her to try to get away, try to hurt me, show me more of her strength and will.

She only straightens her smile to be sweet and innocently whispers, "I'd never want to hurt such a perfect cock, Simon." She licks her lips, lowering her voice even more. "How would you make me come then, baby?" She exaggerates a few blinks of her dark eyes.

I laugh. She's infuriating and frustrating, but damn if I'm not liking that she isn't meek. "Oh? You wanna come for me?"

"Yes, please." She laughs, and her eyes dance between my mouth and my hard dick.

I drag her hands to above her head and take both wrists easily with one of my hands, moving my other arm under her waist and hoisting her up the bed to the headboard. She remains silent, not helping, not resisting.

Lying flat against her side, I can feel her heat again, feel the sweat of our skin cold against each other. I pull my face down to hers and find her lips open and greedy, her tongue fighting for every inch of my mouth. I bite her tip to get her to stop, to yield, but she only arches her neck and pulls her tongue between my teeth, moaning into my mouth. She is a willful little bitch.

I don't let her tongue go, keeping her face pinned to mine. My free hand roams the side of her body, down her ribs, up her hip and thigh, over the skin inflamed by my whip. She wiggles and moans against my teeth, pressing her pussy into me more when I run my fingernails across raised marks. I let go of her tongue finally, pulling my face away and bringing my hand up to her tit. We're both panting, and

I can feel each breath from her tiny frame. Her eyes are glazed with desire, half-open; she wags her tongue at me, showing my teeth marks have claimed her mouth.

I like how my hand completely covers her breast— darker fingers over creamy skin, fingers that I align with the marks of the whip. I gently trace a thicker line from the top of her tit, down around her raised nipple, to the bottom of the small swell.

"Harder." She arches against my touch, pleading the word with a deep moan for me to stop being gentle.

I laugh quietly, continuing to run my fingers across the marks I've given her. It's a feather touch that brings goose bumps and hardens her nipple more. "You like pain, Grace?"

"No." I look into her eyes at her breathy response and can see that she's not playing. She's not lying with this answer. She has the first hint of fear, almost panic, but it's gone before I can savor it.

"But you ask me to hurt you more?" Our voices are so quiet, barely whispers. The yes from her lips is no more than a small sigh. "Why?" I pull away to examine her face more, my own switching between a frown and a smile.

"Because you will anyway, won't you?" Her voice is higher, softer, and her eyes fill with tears. Her scent spikes with the familiar fragrance of fear. Gone is the lust. Fear and pain are all her eyes give me now, and her breath hisses in and out. Her body shrinks away from my touch, pushing deeper into the soft bed. She swallows hard and tries to get her breathing under control. "Please…" But she stops her whimper and closes her eyes, relaxing her body into mine.

I watch, fascinated at her quick changes, not moving. My hand rests on her tit, feeling the subtle shifts in her body as they happen. When her eyes open, her breathing is back to normal again. Her heart rate is slowed again. The tiny tears are blinked onto her lashes, making them prisms to shine against her dark lust-filled eyes. "You do want to hurt me more, don't you, Simon?"

I laugh in response to the obvious want in her voice. "Which is it? You do or don't like pain?"

"It excites me." I can see that I won't get another honest answer out of her. Even her scent is back to normal. Her whole body refuses to give in to the pain and fear I saw for only one moment.

I move my hand to swirl my finger around her tight nipple before pinching and rubbing it between my finger and thumb. "You are amazing." I stare into her eyes as I squeeze harder.

"Thank you." Her voice isn't even strained, just a whisper, a raised eyebrow. Her eyes meet mine calmly.

"How do you have such control over your body, Grace? Who taught you this?" I kiss these words next to her ear, gently brushing my lips down her face and neck. My fingers never let up.

She only smiles more, wiggling her hip against me as I twist her nipple cruelly.

"You know I'm going to break you?" I let her nipple go and rise to my knees over her, still holding her hands above her head.

"I know you want to." Her eyes stare up at me with that softness again. "But I've already been broken, Simon. There's nothing left for you to do but love me or hurt me."

I can't help but laugh at this answer. "You want me to love you, Grace?" The thought crossed my mind that she might be perfect for me, but love isn't something I've felt before. It's not something I'm open to.

She raises her eyes to mine again, and it's the fear I see that takes my breath away as much as her words. "If *you're* not too broken."

Seattle: Miles Vanderson

Gillian came to me in the library that night. I didn't hear her enter, so lost in my own thoughts and the warmth of the room. I didn't know she was there until she stood before me in her usual spot, the fire showing me her body through her long sleep shirt.

We didn't speak, not at first. We hadn't spoken all day, not really. The civilities of dinner conversation, the talking around other people, the uncomfortable silence surrounding her nightly predictions: that was all we shared in terms of words that day. I hadn't had her alone.

But there she was, in front of me. Alone finally. So much had changed between us. The speech I had, my plan, no longer mattered. It did, but it didn't. I hadn't given up my plan, only put it on hold.

I spoke first. Maybe if I had let her go first, things might have been different. I'll never know, and I've given up thinking about that. I've given in to Gillian's belief that we're all guided, either by the stars or fate or karma. What happened was meant to happen.

"You were a naughty girl with your horoscopes tonight." I bring myself out of my reverie to address her, an equal mix of laughter and anger in my voice. I surprise myself with the tone I use. I'm still angry with her for revealing our secrets to her mother. I sound like my father even to myself, authoritative and strong. I've been gentle with Gillian before, but now there's no denying that I'm demanding a response from her. There's no denying that things have changed between us.

She'd remained standing, but her body language changed slightly. She flickered before me. That's how I always thought of Gillian's behavior, flickering, like a hummingbird's wings on the wind. It was so quick and effortless, one long motion from start to finish but hardly visible in between. Or like a movie, one image would just merge into the next. I didn't recognize it then, but I came to know the signs later. I came to understand so much about her later. But that night was just the beginning in so many ways for us.

"Mama done tol' me I's a bad girl." Her voice is shaky, the fire crackling louder than her words. There's an odd lilt to how she sounds too, as though the shame she must feel has an added effect of degrading her speech as well as her stance.

"Yes. You were bad tonight." I sit up and lean towards her, my right hand held out for her to take. She shrinks away, her body bending at the waist, collapsing into her middle. She wraps her arms around herself and falls to the floor on her knees.

I push off the chair and drop to my knees as well, encircling her in my arms, trying to press her to my chest. She's frantic and wild, trying to get away from me, backing into the fireplace, slapping my hands and grunting. "Gillian? ... Gillian! ... Stop!"

In an instant, she's calm again, sitting back on her heels with her hands clasped in her lap. She's the picture of an angel in prayer with the soft glow of the fire on one side of her. Light and dark. It's just like that first time I saw her here.

I pull her face towards mine in a slow lift of my hand to her chin. "Gillian?"

"Yes, Miles?" Her voice is calm, airy.

"Are you all right now?" I know the answer can only be no. After all that's happened today, how could she be okay?

"Yes." She grasps my hand with both of hers. "I've misbehaved tonight, haven't I?" I can't really see her eyes, but I see her lashes blinking quickly, her lids rising and falling. I push her hair back with my free hand to better see her features.

"Why did you write those horoscopes?" I whisper this, almost sorry to give voice to the anxiety I felt listening to her earlier.

"Those horoscopes were written this morning." She raises her voice and face, leaning into me more. "Before you arrived today, Miles." She squeezes my hand harder. "Before you came to my room. I only read what was written for each of us." I'm embarrassed at her mention of this afternoon, at what happened in her room. I know I should be the one making atonement to her.

"But you must have known that it would anger your mother…"

"Yes…" She ducks her head down a little in shame. "Did I anger you, Miles?"

I answer without thinking, a newfound freedom and power. "Yes." And in this moment, I understand something that had been lost on me before. In the bedroom, Anya started the chain of events. She directed my hands, directed Gillian. She punished Gillian in front of me. I stood by and watched, but I also stopped her. I had said when Gillian had enough, and Anya had stopped without question. And when I pushed Anya back on the bed, she didn't resist. I held Anya down while I had sex with her. I took control of Anya. She gave me control of Gillian. And I took it.

"Mother said you were angry with me…that I have to make it up to you." Her little hands over mine squeeze once more before she lets go and rises on her knees more. She takes off her shirt in front of me, appearing just as she was this afternoon, nude and beaten. But now, it's just for me.

Anderson Valley: Simon Lamb

"Watch how you talk to me, Grace. You're dangerously close to pissing me off."

"You *are* broken, aren't you?" Her voice is challenging, but her eyes stay soft, questioning. I release her hands and smack her across the face hard, but not hard enough to leave a mark. I want her face to stay untouched, my marks hidden for only me to see. Her eyes cloud again, the softness replaced by the lust once more.

She doesn't move, just leaves her hands in the same spot I placed them. She remains completely open to me, unfazed even by a second slap.

"What does it take to get to you, to crack through your ice?" I didn't intend to say this out loud. My voice almost cracks with the strained whispering, but I see that my words have more effect than my hands. She turns her face to the side and brings her hands down to cover her chest. Her eyes squeeze closed, and she almost looks like a frightened child, trying to hide from what she fears.

I bring my hand to her face slowly, feathering the side of her cheek with the back of my fingers. My voice is gentle but strong. "Don't hide from me, Grace. It's no use. You're not going anywhere and neither am I. I will break you. You're mine."

My words again have an effect, but not the one I thought they would.

With an animal cry that startles me almost as much as the fist she brings up to jab my throat, Grace moves quickly. I'm pushed off her with the momentum of her movements, not even trying to stop her, still in shock at her sudden change and violence.

Like the cat she so easily imitates, Grace springs to the door. It's locked, an old fashioned door that needs the key to be opened. I watch from my seat on the bed. She releases another animal cry in frustration, turning to face me. My laugh is halted in my throat at the sight of her.

Naked and covered in my whip marks, Grace is beautiful, but her face is stretched into a snarl and her teeth are bared, snapping at me. Her eyes are predatory and darting around the room. Her body is hunched to pounce—a feral and fearless posture. Her breathing is harsh and nasal, a bull before it charges.

"I told you that you're not going anywhere, Red." My words are confident, but I'm not. She's a caged animal and unpredictable right now. She's tiny; I'm not worried about her hurting me, but I don't want her to hurt herself. I don't stop to appreciate the irony of my thoughts.

She ignores my words and circles towards the fireplace, keeping her distance from me. I don't even move from the bed, just watch her. Too late, I realize my error. Grace grabs the fireplace poker and brandishes this as a weapon, holding it like a sword for fencing. She's ridiculously poised with it, like she knows what she's doing. Despite the crazed animal look still on her face, her stance is almost perfect. Her nakedness only enhances her elegance.

"Put that down before you get yourself hurt." I slowly slide to the edge of the bed, not taking my eyes off her. Equally ridiculous, I realize I'm excited by this. My dick is uncomfortably stiff. I stifle a laugh at the image of our two swords facing off.

"Ya likes hurtin' little girls, dontcha mister?" Her voice is deep and gravelly with a hint of a southern accent I haven't noticed. Before I can answer, she attacks me.

She lunges at me with the poker aimed right for my stomach. I barely move out of the way to parry and shove her face first onto the bed, using her forward motion against her. She's quick, but I'm quicker, straddling her back and grabbing her wrists before she can roll over. She lets out one more screech of animalistic frustration and anger as I squeeze her wrists, forcing her to release her grip on the poker. I shove it off the bed and move off her enough to flip her over, not letting go of her wrists.

I straddle her again, keeping her firmly pinned down. I'm amazed at her strength and the fury in her eyes. She doesn't let up, trying to push and pull against me. "Grace, calm down. I'm not going to hurt you. I promise. Calm down!" All I can do is push her harder into the bed.

It's not all I could do. I know I could knock her out. I've done it before as a last resort for subduing a girl. But seeing her irrational fear and wild anger now, after she so calmly and hungrily accepted the pain of my whip moments ago, I'm thrown off guard. I feel an urge I haven't felt in a long time, maybe ever. I *want* to calm her, comfort her. I've done that plenty of times—the equal parts of pain and pleasure needed to break a girl—but with Grace, I feel an urge to protect her too. I *want* to soothe her, to bring her out of this episode of craziness that has seized her. I *want* her to trust me.

I keep talking, trying to lull and ease her back to a calmer state. It's not working, but she is tiring. Finally, her body and face relax. It happens so quickly, I don't let up the pressure on her wrists right away, just stare into her blinking eyes. And they're not blank, not filled with fear or lust, only pain—deep, dark pools of pain.

Yet another version of the woman I've become obsessed with stares back at me. A version that is more raw and hurt than I could ever make her with just my whip. A version that is completely open and vulnerable to me. A version that has me feeling unguarded and exposed. Fuck.

She turns her head to the side, and I watch one small tear slide down her cheek onto the bed.

Seattle: Miles Vanderson

I've judged myself for that day, that night. Many times, I've chastised myself the way anyone else would. How could I do that to my Gillian? How could I continue the madness from that afternoon, now that it was just the two of us, alone? How did I not find a way to end what was only just starting?

But I've given up those thoughts. I've seen the truth for what it was. The only way to get Gillian away from her mother, to free her from her abuse, was to take control. I saw a path in that moment when Gillian was kneeling and naked before me again.

I heard her words from her earlier predictions. She'd said that I was on a precipice, a point of no return, but she hadn't meant that afternoon as I had initially thought. No, she meant that moment between just us that night.

I had a choice to make, and I made it. I *would* be her savior, but not in the way I had originally planned. I would take us down the path, the only path we had open to us. I would lead her and save her. I would keep her.

"You are beautiful, Gillian." My voice catches with the lust I feel, the love I feel. Once again, she takes my hand gently, like that first time. Only now, she doesn't bring it to her lips; she directs my hand to her chest, laying my fingers flat under hers.

"I'm yours, Miles." Her heartbeat and breathing are so steady compared to my own.

"You are mine, and I'll protect you. I'll keep you safe from now on." She smiles at this, her serene, soft smile. "I have a plan for us, my love, a way that we can be together always. Would you like that?"

She nods her head slowly, and without thinking, I move my hand across her skin. This wasn't my plan. My plan had been to wait, but everything changed this afternoon. Anya knows about us, about me. I have to follow this new plan, down to the darkest depths if necessary.

"I'm sorry for making you angry, Miles." Her soft, airy voice cuts into my thoughts, into the soothing feel of her skin against my hand.

"Did your mother tell you to apologize to me?"

"Yes."

"Did she tell you anything else?" I want to forget about Anya. I want to grab Gillian and run away together, but I know I can't. I have to see my new plan through. It will work. It has to for our sake.

"Yes." Gillian pauses, blinking at me. Her heartbeat is so strong and even, it's almost like she's sleepwalking. *"But I don't want to repeat her words."*

"But you have to tell me, Gilli. I need to know what your mother says and does. It's important that you always tell me everything. The truth. I can help, but only if I know what your mother is up to. Do you understand?"

"Yes."

"So tell me the truth."

She pulls away from me, my hand dropping to my own knees. Her body crumples into itself again. Her stomach concaves, shoulders round, and she's rocking back and forth. I can hear her mumbling, see her lips moving.

"Gillian! Look at me." It takes just a moment, a blink of my eyes, for her to straighten up again in response to my sharp tone. She keeps her head lowered though, my angel in prayer.

"I'm to tell you that when I anger her, I'm to be punished. That if you won't punish me, she will. She said that you'll want to from now on." She raises her eyes to me but keeps her chin down. Her straight-faced stare makes me want to cry. "Do you want to, Miles?"

"Yes." I give this whispered confession without hesitation. "But I...I can't." I grab her face with both my hands, pulling her towards me. "I love you, Gillian."

"I love you, Miles."

It was the first time Gillian and I said those words to each other. How perfect that it was in the library. How strange that it was under those circumstances.

I pulled her to me for a kiss, our first real kiss. Only our lips had touched before in almost chaste kisses. The kiss I gave her then was definitely not chaste. I claimed her mouth as mine; I claimed her body as mine with my hands, touching every inch I could reach.

I've blamed myself. I've berated myself for not stopping, for not being strong enough to resist the need I had in that moment.

But I've given up those self-recriminations too. I've long since resigned myself to the fate I sealed for us. I've embraced the memory of her, me, us. I've allowed the dark twists of my thoughts to come to light. I've not hidden behind the small attempt to make myself more innocent in all that happened.

I claimed all of Gillian as my own that night, right there in front of the fire. And I did punish her. I knew it was the only way. I would be gentler than Anya would be should I refuse.

I won't pretend that was my only reason though. I didn't want to wait. I liked the control and power that was mine. And now, in the darkness alone, I can admit as I always do to myself that I liked punishing her. I liked knowing she was all mine, and only I would have her that way from then on.

She didn't cry. She just submitted to me. I held her for hours that night in front of the fire. I enjoyed our peaceful end to a horrific day; it was a beautiful beginning to our lives together.

Anderson Valley: Simon Lamb

I wanted her tears. I wanted her screams. I wanted everything I usually got from a girl I brought here. But her one lonely tear is more than I can take, more than I can handle. "Grace…" I whisper. I don't want to break her calm again. I don't want to startle or scare her more. "Can I let you up? Will you be a good girl?" She only nods once, still keeping her face turned away from me.

I let go of her arms, noting my red finger marks on her tiny wrists. I don't move off her though. I sit up more, taking my weight off her but keeping her between my legs. She doesn't try to move, not even her arms which must be sore from fighting me.

I gently reach out and pull her face back towards me; she doesn't resist. Her eyes are soft and lined with tears, but her voice is strong. She sounds sweeter, softer. "I'm sorry." No seduction, no anger, no fear.

"Wanna tell me why you flipped out?"

She shakes her head but keeps her eyes on mine.

I smile. "I'm used to a girl being afraid or a little freaked out when I use a whip, not when I'm just talking." She returns my smile; hers is more tentative and like a butterfly's wings, spread wide for only a small moment. "Was it a delayed reaction to the whipping?" I glance down at her body. The marks are red and angry looking in spots. Her nipples are painfully erect still. She doesn't follow my look, just stares steadily up at me.

"No. I didn't feel the punishment."

"It wasn't a punishment whipping." I correct her automatically. I decide not to expand on that just yet. "I thought you were enjoying it as much as I was."

"Yes."

I frown at her obvious lie. "You said it excited you."

"Yes." Another lie, but she *was* excited before.

"But now you say you didn't feel it?"

"Yes." Lying again? I don't think so.

I put my hands to my face in frustration. I'm getting nowhere with her. I run my hands through my hair and push a big sigh out, looking down on her again. She hasn't moved or changed expression other than the small smile. "I need you to be honest with me, Grace. I need you to tell me the truth." Her face flinches for a moment, a shadow of the anger peeks through her softness. "Why did *that* just upset you? Can't you be honest with me?"

"Have *you* been honest with me, Simon?"

I smile at this. "Yes. For the most part." And it's true. I didn't lie to her about my intentions in bringing her here.

"What part haven't you been honest about then?"

"You'll answer my questions first, Red."

"Please call me Grace. I like that name better." She lowers her eyes to my mouth. "I like the way it sounds from you."

I smile once more, and her eyes come back to mine. She doesn't return my smile this time, just waits for me to speak.

"All right, Grace." At this, she smiles—a sweet, wide smile that startles me. It's a smile I've only seen when I give a girl an extravagant gift, not after I've just whipped her or when I'm holding her down. I brush my thumb across her soft lips, and she smiles even more for me. I'm distracted from the craziness of a moment ago by her beauty, her openness.

"Why did you freak out? What was it that I said or did that had you so afraid and angry?" I try for a gentle tone, but my natural authority, my naturally controlling tone, comes through anyway.

She swallows hard but bravely doesn't look away. I can see the fear in her eyes again—what I've wanted to see for so long—but this isn't how I wanted it to be. I knew she was broken; that was part of the challenge with her. I had no idea just how broken she was though, and now that she's here—under me, wearing my marks…I don't know what to think. My fucking feelings are getting in the way.

"You said I was yours." Her voice is flat, holding back emotions that her eyes only hint.

"And that made you angry?"

"No." She pauses, looking down at my mouth again for a brief second. "Yes. But mostly afraid."

"Why afraid?" She shakes her head, closing her eyes. "No. Look at me!" Her eyes pop open, and I have a momentary thought that I'm glad she didn't change in that second. She's still soft and open, sweet. I'm able to soften my tone a little. "Why afraid, Grace?" She responds to me using her name, almost smiling.

"I don't belong to you."

I chuckle at this. I look down at her body, pinned under mine. "Yes. You do."

"I can't belong to you when I already belong to another." She shakes with the last word, her eyes pierced with fear, filled with tears. I can smell it on her, feel it from her, and I'm rattled by a stab of jealousy.

I've never felt jealous before. Whatever I've wanted, I've had. I've taken. No woman has been out of my reach unless I placed her there by my own rules. I've stolen women from other men before, just for the fun of it or because I could. It's not a game I play often, too boring and easy, but I've never had a woman refuse me yet. And I've never lost a woman to another man. Even Raquel begged me not to push her away. She said she'd find a way to get out of marrying that other guy. I was the one that ended things with her.

Grace is slightly calmer when she speaks before I can, "I don't want to lead you on, Simon."

I laugh at this, shaking my head at her seriousness. She's whipped, in my home, under my control, and she's worried about leading *me* on?! But she speaks again before I stop laughing, "I can't give you what you want."

I still shake my head, now with equal parts confusion and amusement. "What is it you think I want, Grace?"

"Me. *All* of me."

I grin. "I think I already *have* you right where I want you, sweetheart."

She shakes her head, a look of sadness in her eyes. No. Pity? "You hide almost as much as I do." She laughs at her own words, short but sweet—a soft, sad, tinkling bell sound. I automatically put my hand on the side of her throat to feel it, and she smiles like she understands my need. "I can't give you all of me. It's not mine to give anymore."

She moves finally, lifting one hand off the bed and placing it lightly on my chest. Her fingers are delicate and cool, lightly rubbing just the tips against my skin. My chest pops in goose bumps. "For what it's worth, some of me is already yours. You'll never have all of me though. I'm sorry, Simon."

I react without thinking, grabbing her arms and holding her down again, growling inches from her face. "I have all of you right now, Grace! You're not going anywhere, and you *will* give yourself to me! Whether you try to fight me or not."

She only adds to my anger by smiling sweetly up at me, ignoring the pain in her wrists I must be causing. Her voice is airy and cool. "I'm sorry." She moves her eyes back to the spot she was just touching on my chest. "I wish I could give you what you need, Simon. I wish…" She looks back into my eyes with that look of pity again. "I wish we weren't so broken."

I lose it. I let go of her and backhand her across the mouth hard. Hard enough to break open her lip. Hard enough to see her bright red blood smear across her white teeth. Hard enough to scrape open the skin of my knuckle on her tooth.

I jump off her. I expect her to react with the same wild anger, to charge at me. I hope she will. I want her to hurt me back. I would let her hurt me. I stand, shaking and panting, waiting for her to move. I stand completely open, but she stays on the bed, unmoving. I didn't hit her hard enough to knock her out.

"Grace?" I whisper her name, not stepping towards her. Her hair covers her face; her body lies still and lifeless. Her stomach rises and falls with even breaths, as if in a deep sleep. "Grace." I stand next to the bed, bumping it with my legs. There's no reaction, no movement still.

I sit on the bed and reach slowly towards her face. No change. I brush her hair off to the side, trailing wisps of her blood along her jaw. Her face is still soft, innocent, marred only by the ugliness of my anger. The urge to protect her again shoots pain up my stomach, clenching the air from my lungs. I'm overwhelmed by its suddenness and strength, the unfamiliarity of feeling anything for a girl.

I swallow back the tears I feel stinging my eyes. I lean forward and gently kiss her lips, staining my own with the pain I've caused, with the mark of my shame. One tear falls on her cheek, and I watch it roll to the side to get lost in her hair. It follows the path of her one tear.

I've never lost my temper like that. I've hit women. I've brutalized women, all in the name of the game I play, all calculated and in control. I've been merciless in my demand for complete obedience and submission before, but I've never once lost control of myself. I've never even once been emotional around a woman before.

I gently wipe the spot on her cheek made wet with my tear. I can feel more wanting to escape. Instead, I jump up and head to the bathroom. I avoid looking at myself in the mirrors, avoid turning on a light. I reach for a washcloth and wet it with cold water.

Grace is still as she was on the bed, unmoving. I gently wipe her mouth and face. Her lip is already swelling, but the cut is small at least. I lean down for one more kiss on her cheek and whisper, "I'm sorry, Grace."

I've never apologized for something I've done. I think I apologized to my grandfather once…maybe. I take a deep breath against more tears and stand up, covering Grace with a blanket. I move to sit at the chair next to the fireplace, watching her peaceful breathing.

In Flight: Miles Vanderson

Today will be a good day. Hopefully.

I'm heading to San Francisco to weed through Spencer's latest findings in person. The man has proved worth his weight in gold so far. I know where Gillian has been since she left my house three years ago. Just saying these words to myself is a miracle. Spencer has certainly earned his bonus payment.

I turn my face towards the window to hide my content from the flight attendant. I already told her that I didn't need anything else, but she's been back to pester me a few times. She's pretty enough and her blowjobs are nice, but I'll have to replace her. I can't have staff around that doesn't follow my expressed wishes.

I go back to thinking more about Gillian, smiling to myself. I know she has a small apartment. So she's living with a boyfriend but not permanently. More importantly, she didn't leave me to be with him.

The thought didn't really cross my mind for more than a second. Gillian didn't even have any contact with anyone outside of my home for the last year she was with me. I kept her fairly hidden away. She was all for me alone. So I knew from the start that she hadn't run away to be with another man.

I still don't understand why she ran when things were so settled between us. She'll be able to explain it herself soon enough though. Hopefully, today. Such a nice thought. I'll have Gillian with me, where she belongs, today.

Spencer said she's been modeling. I try to envision this. My Gillian, so shy and quiet, a model? He sent me a few samples of her work. I force myself not to think about the more pornographic ones. She was nearly nude in some of them. I try not to imagine finding her on some lewd modeling job today.

It no longer matters. I'll purchase the rights to any images of her. No one else will ever see them again. Gillian really should know better than to put herself on display for just anyone to see. Maybe it's just another way of acting out, rebelling against me?

Her eyes in a few of the photos are still haunting me. I know the looks. I know all of her looks. All the incarnations of my Gillian. She can't hide from me, not any longer.

She'll learn soon enough what happens when she tries to run and hide. She'll learn what all her acting out and rebelling has earned her. I smile contentedly at these thoughts. Hopefully, today.

I'll fire the flight attendant when we land. I don't want her on the flight back with Gillian and me. I won't want any distractions then.

Anderson Valley: Simon Lamb

"Mr. Simon?" It takes me a minute to realize where I am, to fully open my eyes. To remember yesterday.

There's another knock on my bedroom door as I look down at my feet. Grace is curled against my legs, sitting on the floor with her cheek pressed to my knee. My hand is buried in her hair. She's wrapped in the blanket I used last night to cover her. I don't know when she moved from the bed to the floor.

I clear my throat, and Grace slowly raises her head to look at me. She's soft and pretty except for the side of her mouth. I wince when her attempt to smile stops with a small frown.

I'm stiff from sitting all night in the chair, but I gently move my leg from behind her to stand. "Don't move."

I quietly grab the key from a side dresser. When I turn the knob to open it, a servant is just turning away. "Good morning, Hillary." I keep the door mostly closed, hiding my naked lower body behind it. I no longer take my sadistic pleasures out on the staff. I stopped that childish behavior long ago, but I'm also acutely aware of Grace behind me.

"Sorry to disturb you, Sir. Will you be coming down for breakfast, or would you like it served in here this morning?"

I glance back at Grace, sitting motionless on the floor. "Please serve on the upstairs veranda. We'll be there in thirty minutes."

She nods and walks quickly away. My staff is used to my routine. That's why she was knocking; I never sleep in this late. I close the door but don't lock it again.

Turning slowly back to Grace, I'm suddenly nervous. Yesterday didn't go at all how I'd intended. Last night was a disaster. I have no idea how she'll be this morning, despite waking to find her sitting at my heels like a loyal pet.

I watched her till late in the night. I don't know what time I finally fell asleep, but it was after a long time thinking about her.

I was honest with myself. I admitted that I didn't want to treat Grace like the usual girl I bring here. From the start—not putting her in the trunk, having her join me for a nice dinner—it wasn't a girl's typical first day here with me. I couldn't pinpoint the moment, though, that she went from a girl I want to train to a girl I just want. When she went from a girl I want to hurt for my own pleasure to a girl I cried over.

It disturbed me. It still does. I don't like feeling out of control, yet I was with her. I don't like going against my routines and plans, yet I have with her every time I've been near her.

I cried over her! Fuck. That just doesn't happen to me. I'm still shaken this morning, still unsure of what to do. I stay against the door, only watching her. She watches me back with her eyes wide and barely blinking.

I came to terms with what made me angry last night too. Grace didn't respond how I expected. She was perfect in yielding to my whipping her, but she was a pain in the ass when it came to getting anything else from her. She showed that she was willing to be completely submissive to me, but she refused to show any fear or pain doing it. She went from strong and challenging to soft and sweet in the blink of an eye. Oh, and to homicidal fencing pro too. I glance over at the poker still on the floor. Grace doesn't follow my eyes, just keeps looking up at me.

It wasn't her attempt to hurt me that angered me though. I liked that she was fighting me. It wasn't her refusal to give me any sign of fear either. Her excitement only fueled my own. For the first time, I felt I had a woman under my control that could truly appreciate my darkest desires, match them with her own even.

I never knew what was missing from all of the other products I trained for other men. It wasn't the submission because that was always there, same as their fear and pain. I thought those were what I craved. With Grace, I had her submission without fear or pain. I had her compliance, her like-mindedness, a thirst for what only I could quench. And Grace was craving for more. *I* wanted more.

I only became angry when she was soft and sweet and open, insisting that *I* was broken. It was an instant and unfamiliar reaction. I felt too defenseless by her words. She's obviously crazy, obviously broken, yet *she* was pitying *me*?! I can feel myself getting angry again just standing here, angry and more uncertain—more unfamiliar feelings again.

Her mercurial changes in behavior are beyond crazy. I should drive her back to the city and dump her. I should just forget about her, but the thought makes my stomach flip-flop. The thought that she'll want to leave this morning has the same effect. I won't *let* her go, but I want her to *want* to stay with me. I want the woman that craves my same desires and the one that brings out this unfamiliar openness in me.

I have no idea what to say to her. Plenty I could say, like "you're right, I'm a messed up prick that's never had a close relationship with anyone or anything." Or "sorry about the welts and broken lip; can we start over?" Fuck.

"Good morning, Simon." Her voice is clear and sweet. She's beautiful—still no hint of fear or pain. She moves her hand out from under the blanket and tentatively touches her lip, with just her fingertips though.

"Sorry about that." I can't believe I'm apologizing again. Maybe because I hurt her unintentionally? Out of uncontrolled anger? Go ahead, tough guy, say it. Out of unfamiliar fear. I was angry with her because I was afraid she was right. That I *am* too broken to be with her.

"You already apologized last night." But she's not looking back up at me. Her cheeks flame red.

"I thought you were asleep." Or passed out.

"I heard you." Her eyes lift to me, and I have an unsettling urge to drop to my knees and beg her forgiveness over and over. What the fuck is wrong with me? "I thought you brought me here to enslave me?"

"I did." I want to say that I've changed my mind, but I don't because I haven't made up my mind. I don't know if I want her around at all if it means being out of control.

"Yet you apologize when you hurt me?"

"I'm not apologizing for the rest of it. Just that." I at least sound convincing.

She seems to remember that her body is peppered with whip marks, like she didn't feel them before I mentioned it. She lowers the blanket to fan out around herself, revealing red and swollen lines across her upper body. Her hair hides some, but her tits are obviously a mess of welts. I wince again, seeing what I did to her.

And I'm hard.

I'm awkwardly aware of being nude again. I look around but don't see any way of covering without making it obvious that I'm self-conscious right now. I look back at Grace, and she's watching me with a strange look on her face. It's like she can see right through me. I'm too open to her, too exposed.

She rises on her knees and moves the blanket further off herself. I can see more marks lining her stomach and legs, but she's moving so lithely and smoothly, without any sign of pain; I'm distracted watching her.

Before I realize her intentions, she's crawling on all fours to me, tentative at first, looking to see if I'll stop her. I don't say anything, transfixed with watching her cat crawl to me. When she's inches away, she stops, rising on her knees. Her hands reach slowly out, still watching to see if I'll halt her; she takes my hard dick in her cool and gentle hands.

I have a brief thought that she could be planning to hurt me and try to escape, but her eyes tell a different story. It's not her seductive, mischievous look from before. There's a hint of something close to wanting, lust that is undeniable. I almost moan seeing it. That and her hands are ringing up and down my cock, twisting the shaft and pulling on my balls with the most perfect gentle pressure and gliding.

"Grace…" I can't believe I'm going to tell her to stop, but I think we need to talk. In a minute maybe. My stomach clenches when she slides a finger up and over the wet tip.

"May I?" I feel her gently pulling my cock towards her open mouth, but the sight of her cracked lip and bruised face is enough to shake me out of the moment.

I put my hands on her shoulders. "Grace, your mouth…"

She ignores this and puts the tip of me between her lips. I can feel the warmth of her breath before she flicks her tongue out to tease the opening, to trace around the top. Her mouth wraps around me, and I let out a long moan as she pulls more of me into her.

She's gentle, pushing her tongue on me with a soft pressure. She doesn't take me as deep, but her tongue runs up and down every inch and her hands glide over me. I can feel myself getting close to coming, but I want more of her.

I gently pull her head away, and she gives me her sweet, soft smile. On her knees, covered in my marks, but with the most angelic and sweet face, she's perfect. I help her stand, and she turns to quickly crawl on the bed, lying down with her arms outstretched for me. I have a crazy thought about wanting to make love to her. Not just sex, not just fucking hard like we've done so far, but giving her something more to keep her smiling so sweetly at me, to keep her soft and open for me.

I crawl in between her open legs and wrap my arms around her as she does the same to me. I enter her very slowly and gently. Her little moan is high pitched and soft in my ear. I stay close to her, keeping our bodies pressed hard, just my hips rock into her. Her legs wrap around mine, pushing herself up and down with me. "Grace, come for me, baby."

"Yes, Simon." Her soft voice, so sweet and submissive, is almost lost in her moans. Her whole body tenses under and around me. I tense too, feeling my own need mounting, my own moan bursting out of me just as we come together. I keep pushing my hips until her moans turn into soft mews and her lips feather against my neck. I pull out as gently as I entered and move off to her side, but I keep her pressed against me, pulling her onto my chest. Our embrace is tight. Our breathing slows together.

"You are a complex girl, Grace." I lazily twirl her hair against her head, liking the feel of its silkiness against my rough hands. "I'm still trying to figure you out. I don't think I ever will." I admit this quietly. I don't add that I don't care if I ever do as long as she stays with me.

She smiles, kissing my chest. "Probably not. You are a conflicted man, Simon." I can't argue with that.

"Are you hungry?" She nods. "Good. Get cleaned up and dressed quickly." I pull my arm from under her and swing my legs off the bed.

She responds quickly, "Yes, Sir." I turn around and she salutes me with a grin, but I can see the underlying layer of submission; she means it too. Like her crawling to me and asking permission to suck me, this is her way of showing her willingness to continue the submission she gave me yesterday. It's not the match to my darker desires, but a match to my obvious need for control. This is her offer to give the equal parts that I need from her. I'm still confused by her, by my reactions to her. In so many ways.

"Grace...do you want to stay here with me?" I'm glad that I was able to keep the weakness out of my voice. Still, I sound husky and raw, like the words are hard for me to say.

She nods, kneeling on the bed, her hands between her legs—the picture of submission. "Do *you* want me to stay, Simon?" Her voice sounds sweet and hopeful.

I nod too. "Let's talk more over breakfast, sweetheart. Get dressed."

Breakfast is a strange ordeal. The warm sunshine and flowering trees don't do their usual magic on my mood. The mix of my unfamiliar embarrassment over Grace's fat lip and our awkwardness with each other far outweigh the surrounding beauty.

I try to avoid seeing the staff stare at her, then me. I can feel my face heat every time I glance at her mouth stretched for a bite. The bruise is only uglier in the bright sun.

I'm shocked that this doesn't have the usual effect on me either. I liked seeing the whip marks. I was obviously turned on by those as usual. Seeing her face battered though…it has the opposite effect. I stop even trying to eat, just sip my coffee and quietly watch her. I'm lost in thinking my thoughts, the same ones from last night.

Grace is oblivious to anyone else. Her odd breakfast habits keep her focused on her plate of pancakes. She didn't have anything to doodle with, so she played with the fruit plate instead. She turned orange slices and strawberries into happy faces, bananas slices and blueberries into sailboats and oceans.

I thought about not letting her, but she seemed so happy. I stopped caring about what the staff thought and just enjoyed watching her strange ritual. At least she isn't upset with me. She completely ignores the marks I left on her. She doesn't seem to feel her swollen lip at all when she takes big bites of syrupy pancake.

When she is finally finished, she slowly lowers her silverware just like yesterday. Grace looks up at me for the first time since sitting down at my table. I dismiss the staff so we can talk in private.

She smiles at me, wiping her mouth gently. She seems to finally feel the pain from her lip. I frown watching her dab at her mouth with a wet napkin, but she speaks before I can say anything. "Please don't apologize again, Simon. I know you're sorry."

"But I want to say I'm sorry over and over until you're healed, Grace!" And I'm shocked, not just at the words, but that I mean them. The same damn emotions from last night are choking my words this morning.

"You mean that." It's not a question. She's surprised by it too. "I thought you were into hurting women…that you liked it."

I let out the breath I was holding. "Yes. That's true." I take her hand over the table; it's sticky from the fruit. "I told you part of the truth yesterday. I bring women here to break them, train them, sell them. I've done this to about twenty women over the past four years." I don't know why I'm telling her this. Making amends? I don't care. Her eyes remain soft—no shock, no fear, no judgment.

"I was going to do this to you when I first saw you."
For some reason, I hesitate to say that I saw her over a year
ago when she was hiding, that I know about her two lives. I
instinctively think this would be what would frighten her.

Her face remains impassive, calm. She even smiles at
me as I continue, "I am sadistic. I was honest yesterday
when I said that." I glance down at the deep V of her shirt; a
few whip marks are visible. "I liked whipping you. I liked
how excited it made you too, but I enjoy it usually even if
the girl doesn't." Again, I'm shocked at my own honesty, at
how calmly I'm admitting this to her, and at how calmly
she's taking it. "So, yes, I like to cause pain, to see what I've
done…usually. But…" I falter trying to make sense of my
thoughts and these fucking churned up emotions.

"But you regret hurting me like this." It's another non-
question. Her eyes are searching mine though, looking for
confirmation. I can only nod and squeeze her fingers. "I
appreciate your honesty. I understand the difference between
your hurting my body for sexual pleasure versus out of fear."

I shake my head in surprise at her clinical tone, like the
pain happened to someone else or she read about it in a
report. Then I realize she said I acted out of fear. I frown,
taking my hand back. "I wasn't *afraid*, Grace. You weren't
going to be able to hurt me, not unless I let you."

"I know you weren't reacting to the silliness with the
poker, but you *were* frightened when I said you were broken
too." This time she doesn't look for a confirmation. She only
sits back and rubs her hands more with the napkin, not
looking at me at all.

"And I told you yesterday to watch how you speak to me." She's hitting too close to the truth, to the frightening feel of being overly exposed around her. I feel like I can't hide anything from her, like I don't even want to. Fuck.

She looks up, wide-eyed and sarcastic. "Oh. Are we done being honest with each other then?" It's the first sign of her not being completely submissive. But she's still soft, still *her*.

I shake my head at my crazy thoughts. She's right. I won't admit to being afraid, but I do want answers from her. "No. I have more questions for you."

"Okay. I'll do my best to answer them then…as long as you do the same." She sits up and puts her hands flat on the table. Her face is composed still, but I can see a shadow to her eyes, a pulling back of her open, soft expression.

"You said you have a safeword, but you've never used it. How many Masters have you had?"

She frowns, shaking her head, obviously uncomfortable with the word. "I had one boyfriend once that called himself that. He said I needed a word, so I gave him one. It was over quickly. Why does being broken frighten you so much?" She doesn't miss a beat.

"Because I've been told before that what I like, what I want, isn't normal." I laugh at myself. "Of course, selling women isn't normal, at least in this country, but I don't think I'm broken just because I like things rough." Before she can respond, I direct a question back to her. "So this boyfriend of yours taught you to submit and take a lot of pain?"

"No. He didn't." Her pause isn't long. "I don't think you're broken for liking rough sex, Simon. I think you're broken because even the thought of loving someone is enough to scare you. Have you ever been in love?"

"No. I haven't." I cock an eyebrow at her. Two can play at the short answers. I don't argue with her assessment either though. "But you *can* take a lot of pain. You were perfect yesterday while I whipped you." She smiles at this, like I just praised her for a job well done. "So who taught you that?" She only shakes her head. "You're not going to answer me?"

She nods slightly. "I'm sorry, Simon. I can't." But this doesn't stop her from asking her own question, "Why did you pick me?"

"Because *you* were so obviously broken. I liked the challenge." She isn't shocked by my answer, only nods like this is what she thought already. "You said you belong to someone else. Who?"

She shakes her head again, a look of regret on her face. "I guess I can't reciprocate your honesty after all."

"So no more questions?"

"It wouldn't be fair if you answer all of mine, and I can't answer any of yours." I laugh at her earnest reply. She doesn't laugh with me.

"And being fair is important to you, Grace?"

"Yes."

"Why? Because life's been unfair to you?"

"Something like that."

"So you won't tell me about your training or who you belong to... Do you love him?" I stop myself from holding my breath; I brace myself to not react one way or another to her answer. Jealousy is new for me but controlling myself isn't.

"Yes. And no."

"Which is it? Yes *or* no?"

"It's not that simple."

"It never is, sweetheart." Before she can reply, I interrupt, "Does he live around here?"

"No. Why do you care if I love someone else?" I'm thrown by how she continues to challenge me, I had expected her to back down by now.

"Who says I care?"

She only raises her eyebrow to this answer. "What makes you think *I'm* broken?"

I laugh again. "You're kidding, right?" She shakes her head. I debate telling her that I know about her time in Chinatown, that I have a theory about her. I decide to skirt this for now. "You were fucking your boyfriend's brother *and* me." Her face flushes with embarrassment, and she looks down quickly. I lean forward to touch her blush, to feel her warmth. I want to kiss her cheek, but I resist. Her eyes are startled up to mine at my gentle touch. I smile and add, "I'm not judging, Grace." She returns my smile with only a small upturn of her lips. I frown at her bruised face, feeling my own embarrassment, saying quieter, "I believe it's your turn."

"Why are you being so nice to me now, Simon?"

"Who says I am?" I grin but quickly add, "I want you to stay." Her smile is the same as last night, like I just gave her the biggest, most expensive present she's ever received. "I want to know more about you." And it's gone just like that, replaced with a deep frown.

I decide to press my luck. "I think you hide yourself away, and I don't want you to do that with me. I want to know all of you."

She shakes her head, sad. "I told you last night, I can't give you all of me."

"Why not? Because you belong to some asshole that hurt you? Are you running from him? Is that why you're hiding?" I know I've pushed her too far.

I lean forward, looking into her eyes as they slowly blank, the color becoming darker. Her face relaxes even more and in a blink, she's stretching. A spell broken. Arms high above her head, one hand caresses down the other arm to her shoulder. Her free hand falls to fluff her hair—a cat primping in the sunshine. Her eyes sparkle, and her mischievous wicked grin is back, a little off kilter from the swelling.

She brings her fingers up to her lip, touching lightly. Her tongue darts out to run over the broken skin. "Jesus, Trust." It's the oddest thing to watch, like it's the first time she's realizing I hit her.

"I'm sorry," I say again but this time with a flat tone, studying her reaction.

"You should be!"

I frown, continuing in the same flat tone, hiding any reaction, "You just said you didn't want me to apologize more."

"Oh." She squints at me before waving her hand in the air. "Well, I can say some pretty stupid shit sometimes. I think you should get down on your knees and beg my forgiveness for messing up my pretty face. I have a job in a few days, and this is going to look like crap on camera." She manages a good pout despite the swelling, or maybe because of it.

"Not going to happen, Red." My voice is still flat, but I'm getting excited. I'm getting used to seeing her quick change in behavior, but it's still startling in its extremes. "I told you that you're not leaving here, and *you* said you wanted to stay anyway."

I took a psychology class in college and became pretty fascinated with abnormal behavior for a while. Maybe it was from being forced to see a shrink when I was a teenager. I liked finding out how little is known about the human psyche. The shrinks want to all act like they have everything figured out, but the reality is they don't know shit either.

I continued long after the class to research on my own. I learned many useful tips on conditioning. I learned even more useful tips about selecting the right girls for myself and others.

Grace's behavior is textbook abnormal, but I'm still not sure I believe what I'm seeing. Or what I think I'm seeing anyway. It would explain a few things. I started speculating last night while I watched her sleep. My crazy ass theory has solidified this morning, talking to her.

"Well, I'm not going to stay if this is how you're going to treat me." She rises to stand, glaring at me. Her hands are firmly planted on the table though.

"Sit down, Red. Or I'll take my belt to you right here." I lower my hand to the top of my shorts. I watch for her reaction, making a bet with myself about it.

Her smile twitches, and her fingers tap against the table. "All right, but only because you asked so nicely." She slowly sits back down, pushing her chair back and crossing her legs dramatically. I can't help but notice that her hands run up and down her legs, over her thighs and hips. She's teasing and tempting again.

I'm starting to think of this version as Red and the other version as Grace. Versions? Fuck. I don't know what I'm getting myself into. I'm excited, though, and oddly aroused again.

San Francisco: Miles Vanderson

"I'll go in alone." I don't glance at Spencer standing behind me as I turn the knob to the unlocked front door. He's already determined that Gillian isn't here.

"Of course, Sir." He backs off and turns to walk down the hall. "I'll keep an eye out downstairs, just in case she returns."

I tersely nod in agreement, frustrated. I enter Gillian's apartment and close the door quietly, taking a moment to breathe in the scent before looking around. The place is bright with a view of the city down the steep hill out of the large windows. It's all white with primary colors punching the eyes in accents everywhere. She favors red still in the pillows and curtains, and it's practically a forest with plants strewn all around.

Spencer said she hasn't been here in weeks, but she obviously has a service to take care of everything. Gillian was obsessively neat unless she was on one of her rampages, but those were always brief.

I smile with this thought. I was always able to get her out of those fairly quickly. She usually calmed fast enough when I strapped her down to her bed.

I walk to the frames hanging over the white sectional sofa. The childish drawing of a park and houses draws my attention. After her mother died, I allowed her to put up a few of these in her bedroom, but not anywhere that could be seen by anyone else.

Seeing the evidence of her here only adds to my frustration. Spencer said that he hasn't seen her in person yet. He doesn't technically know where she is at the moment. She had some sort of falling out with the boyfriend and hasn't returned to his apartment or here. He's assured me that he'll find her quickly.

I worry, though, that she's lost in another personification of herself. These never last very long, but I'm still concerned that it will delay finding her. I haven't shared this information with any of the investigators before, fearing it would tarnish our future happiness once she was found, but now may be the time to clue Spencer in on her unusual state of mind. I won't lose her again, not when I'm so close to finding her. If I have to reveal a few family secrets, so be it.

I turn to the door of her bedroom. All is perfect here too. I frown at the clothes hanging in her closet, all too tight and revealing for her. They're borderline indecent, reminding me of her horrifying job as a model. No matter. She won't need any of this once she's back where she belongs.

I sit on her bed and make a mental checklist of all that needs to be done. I can feel her close, and this excites me but also steadies my mind again. I've been in a fugue of misery since she ran. Now, I can think clearly again.

On her nightstand is a large, hardbound book of astrology signs for lovers. She hasn't changed much at least. I turn to the page for *Taurus Woman/Aries Man* and rip it out, scrawling across the top

"Gillian – Our stars align again at last, my love. – Miles"

I smile imagining the panic this little note will create for her. I leave the page propped against her pillow. She'll try to run, but she won't escape. Not this time.

I head out of the apartment, closing the door quietly after one last look. I won't return here. Gillian will be brought to me at my hotel suite. Hopefully, soon.

Downstairs, Spencer is pacing the sidewalk across the street. The large bouldered wall of rock behind him rises to a jagged peak with a house perched on top. This part of the city is safer than most when it comes to earthquakes, but the homes all still look precariously hanging onto the hills to me, leaning against each other for support. I hope not to be staying long enough to feel a quake myself.

"Hire whatever staff you need to keep an eye on this place and the boyfriend's apartment, as well as any other locations you know she frequents." Spencer nods. I turn to the open car door; the driver waits silently. "And when she shows up, I want her detained. She is not to be left alone. Tie her up, cuff her, strap her down, drug her, whatever is necessary," I turn to Spencer to finish my statement. His brows are raised, but he doesn't say anything. "Just do not let her get away." I don't wait for his response, only get in the backseat. "Ride along with me, Spencer. I have a few other things to discuss with you as well."

Anderson Valley: Simon Lamb

I silently congratulate myself on being right. Red responds to the rough shit. She's pure sex—rough, hot sex. This is the version I saw downtown, the version of her that fucked me without even stopping to get my name, the version that got so excited when I whipped her last night. This version matches my darker desires perfectly.

I grin and she grins back, reaching across the table to grab my arm. Her hand's still a little sticky, but we both ignore this. "Why don't we go back to bed, Trust?"

"All right." I stand and pull her up to press her body against mine. I have a fleeting insane thought. Is this considered cheating? I laugh and she looks up at me, touching my lips with her fingertip. She tastes like fruit and syrup. I turn around and grab the syrup from the table. She cocks an eyebrow at me but doesn't say a word as I lead her back to my room.

I lock the door behind me but put the key back in the same spot on the dresser. Turning around, I see her standing in the middle of the floor. She's watching me, waiting.

I walk around her to the bed, putting the syrup on the nightstand. I frown looking at the sheets, remembering the sweet smile she had for me this morning, but this is different. This time isn't about sweetness. Red isn't about sweetness. This is insane! I should stop right now and get her to a doctor.

"Take your clothes off, Red." I can hear her following my order behind me. I'm a bad, bad man.

I turn around. She's still just standing and watching, but she's beautifully naked now. I'm shocked by how dramatically different she is from the girl this morning. Grace was sweet, tentative, gentle, soft. She seemed smaller and everything about her was tender. She wasn't weak, but she was submissive. That version pried me open with her softness and forced me to accept the craving to feel more with her than I've ever felt with anyone. She was the version I'm afraid will wade with me into unfamiliar waters of deeper emotions.

Now she's all angles and hard lines. She stands with her hands on her hips, jutting out her body to show off. Her lips are wet and slightly apart, not quite shaped into a smile. And her eyes move over my body slowly. This is a woman who knows what she wants and just how to get it, a polar opposite from this morning. This is the version I want to take deeper into the darkness I've always known and craved. She's the version I know will all too willingly force me into more familiar waters of sadistic desires.

I'm almost kicking myself for not seeing it sooner. I imagined all sorts of crazy stories to explain Grace, but multiple personalities was too crazy to even be on my radar. Now, it seems so obvious.

"Grace?"

She smiles. "Simon?"

"No, I mean…" Fuck. This is going to sound insane if I'm wrong. "Should I call you Red or Grace?"

She only smiles more, cocking her eyebrow and hip at me. "Call me whatever the fuck you like, Trust."

This is getting me nowhere. I have to know if my theory is right. I can't just keep going on like this with her. My cock doesn't agree. I'm hard just looking at her, and her frank desire and bold words only make me want her more.

But I'm not a monster. I've had women under my control for as long as I can remember, but I have rules. I don't take advantage of girls too young or too weak. I suppose I should add "no crazies" to my list now.

What I felt for her last night and this morning was real. I wanted to comfort her, to protect her. I move my eyes over her whipped body and bruised face. Okay. So I don't mean protect her in the traditional sense. I laugh at my whirling thoughts.

She frowns. "Wanna let me in on the joke?"

I move into my bathroom and come back with my robe. "Put this on." She frowns more but takes it from me, holding it against herself. "I don't know exactly how this works, but I need to talk to you. To Grace." She continues to frown at me, not putting the robe on, not moving.

"So talk."

"No." Here goes nothing. "I don't think you're the right one to have this conversation with." I sound like the nutjob here.

She looks around the room, laughing. "Well, I'm all ya got, so shoot."

"I think I know what's wrong with you, Grace. I want to help."

She drops the robe. "I think the only thing wrong here is that I'm naked and you're not, Trust."

"I know about your apartments in Chinatown and Potrero and your job in the Castro, Grace." This does it.

She blanches like I hit her again. Her eyes become completely impassive; her body stiffens. I can only stare, fascinated with the quick and subtle change to her. I think for a second that she's fainting as she collapses onto the floor, but she steadies herself. She stands back up with the robe in her hand, putting it on without looking at me.

She turns away and perches on the chair I spent the night in, her hands clasped in her lap, her chin lowered. I have no idea where to begin. My mind is going to a million places at once.

I sit on the bed. "Grace?"

She still won't look up. "How do you know about all that?"

"I first saw you over a year ago. I followed you. I told you it's what I do. I was going to grab you and bring you here." That all seems like so long ago, like we were both two different people then.

"To sell me." She looks up. Her eyes are bright but no tears fall. She's amazingly quiet and soft. I'm the one that's a coiled up mess of tense muscles and clenched fists. I'm trapped in her steady gaze.

"Yes." Only when she looks back down am I able to speak again. "I lost you when you didn't return to Chinatown. It wasn't until I saw you again, randomly, that I knew about your place in Potrero. I tried to find out more about you, but you're pretty good at hiding." She smiles slightly.

"Not good enough apparently."

"I didn't figure out the rest until this morning."

"The rest?" Her eyes slowly look up. The fear I thought I wanted to see has her breathing a little heavier. Now, I'd give anything to make it go away, but I have to know.

I can hear myself saying the words, as crazy as they are, "Your different personalities."

She looks back down. "Oh. That."

I laugh. I expected her to deny it or call me nuts or jump up like the wild animal she was yesterday. "I'm right, aren't I?"

Her voice is so quiet, but she finally breathes out, "Yes."

I bring my hands up to the sides of my head, staring at the ceiling. I'm frozen like this for a long time. I can't even get my thoughts to stop bouncing around. I had a theory; I examined all the things I knew about her last night, but I couldn't imagine what it would mean if I was right. I finally pull my hands away when Grace stands up. She moves slowly and with tiny steps, like she's waiting for me to stop her. I just watch her as she gets closer.

She finally sits down next to me, putting her hand over mine gently. I had one thought last night and today that kept circling all the others. I tell her before she has a chance to say anything, "I want you to stay." Her hand squeezes mine.

"You can't."

I laugh a harsh, low rattling of my automatic response, "Don't ever tell me what I can or can't do, Grace." I rub my thumb over her fingers. "You said you wanted to stay."

"That was before…"

"I told you that I wouldn't give you a choice." And I still mean it.

"That was before too…"

"Well, nothing's changed." I'm glad that my voice is back to sounding strong and commanding at least.

She looks up at me and smiles. "You're a bad liar, Simon. Everything's changed, and you know it. You don't want me here. How could you?"

I turn to her more, putting both my hands to the sides of her face. "I do want you. I said that this morning *after* I'd already figured you out."

"You want me as your slave."

I smile at how the word sounds from her sweet mouth. I let her face go. Taking her hand instead, I avoid answering her. I'll need more time to figure out what all this means, what her staying would mean for us. "I want to help you."

"I don't need your help."

I laugh again. "You think you can go around bouncing between different homes, being different people...for how long?"

"I can take care of myself, Simon."

"You were living in a rat hole as one person and fucking everything that moved as another." I say this louder than I intended. She recoils and tries to take her hand away, getting up. I grab her wrist and yank her back onto the bed. "I'm not judging, Grace." She stops trying to pull away, but she won't meet my eyes.

When she's sitting quietly again, I ask the questions that have been racking my brain. The ones that I thought about last night, remembering the small amount I learned in psych class. "Do you have any control over it? How long are you able to stay one personality? Do you all know about each other?"

She laughs this time. "I have some control. More since…" But she doesn't finish. "I've had more control over the last few years. For the most part, we know each other pretty well."

"Have you seen a doctor?" I keep thinking that I should be getting her to one, not sitting on my bed chatting about it.

"Yes. It helped. A little anyway."

"Is *this* the real you or is Red?"

She laughs again. I'm still startled at how calm she looks during this insane conversation, how calm I am. "Both. Neither. We're both just a part and whole on our own."

"Do you know how many...you are?" Wow. It just keeps getting crazier.

"Five." Because she's watching me closely, I keep my shock in check. "I think you've met all of us."

I think back to each encounter with her. I think she's right. I have seen five distinctly different versions of her. "When did this start?"

"I've always been like this. We have been five since I can remember. I've always had the others to…to step out when needed."

"To protect you?"

"We protect each other." The craziest part is this makes sense to me. I remember that this disorder usually stems from early abuse. A strong mind will protect itself, splitting to compartmentalize the experiences. It was one of the abnormal behaviors that I found most fascinating when I was in school—how a person without any hope of survival can survive even the worst conditions at any age.

"Why did you agree to come here, to be with me, Grace?"

Her sweet smile. "We like you."

"But I told you that I'm not nice. I warned you. I told you what I planned to do to you." Her smile doesn't change. "Look at how I hurt you already."

"You didn't hurt me this morning, Simon. And you've asked me to stay."

"Yes. But I think for your own good, you *should* leave. I want you to stay, but *I* can't be good for you." She shakes her head, and I pull her face towards to me, keeping her from moving. "You should be in the care of a doctor, not a sadist."

Her fingers are cool when she covers my hands with her own, her sweet smile is replaced with a determined look. "I'm through with doctors, and I'm through running. I will stay if you'll still have us."

"You've been hurt enough, Grace." I get up, needing the distance from her to say what I know I must. "And I'm not the guy you think I am. I didn't hurt you this morning, yes, but that doesn't change who I am. I *like* causing pain. That's not going to change."

"I know that." Her wide-eyed look is so fucking sweet, it hurts for me to look at her. "I'm not asking you to change. Are you asking us to?"

I laugh at the question. It's like the start of a bad joke. The sadist and the crazy chick walk into a bar…

"I've only just figured you out, Grace. Hell, I don't even know your real name. I'm not asking you to change. I wouldn't, but I can't ask you to stay here and…." I don't finish what I was going to say. The words 'and take my abuse' die in my mouth.

I've never really thought of what I do as abuse. Sure, I've kidnapped and tortured women, but in the end, they've been better off. Luanne was starving and living in a dump without power when I found her. She was days away from being evicted and killed by a crazy ex-husband she never would've been able to get far enough away from on her own. She's much better off as Troy's toy. She has everything she'd ever want. And it's all thanks to me seeing her potential as a perfect submissive for a man who could pay any amount to have exactly what he wants.

I've never been wrong about a girl. It's a special gift, I suppose. I've always been able to pick the ones that truly want and need to be dominated. All of my products leave me with a deep understanding of their innate need to succumb to their dark desires; each one understands that my training, no matter how cruel, only brought out those desires.

Raquel was unfortunate. I didn't kill her. I just failed to see how fucked up she was. She was my first after all. I learned from my mistake.

Grace is *obviously* fucked up, and I can't do this to her. I said I wouldn't give her a choice, and I won't.

"I want to stay with you, Simon. *We* want to stay." I laugh at how crazy she sounds, how crazy all of this sounds.

"Too bad. Get dressed. I'm taking you back to the city."

San Francisco: Miles Vanderson

Work is a distraction. I stare down at the reports on the table, but the charts and numbers have lost meaning for me today. Maybe this was why my father threw all of himself into work. He needed to stay distracted from his crumbling dreams.

My own dream of finding Gillian and returning home quickly is proving to be just that, a dream. Spencer and his team haven't found her. He has a lead, the boyfriend's brother. Yet another lead!

The tension in my neck is getting worse again. I rub the spot and walk to the windows. I'm tired of the view in this city. I miss the peace and quiet of the northern woods, but I refuse to leave here without her. I was so certain when I came here that I'd have Gillian back where she belongs. I have to hold on to that certainty.

Of course, I was also confident that she was happy with me. I believed her lies when she professed her love for me. I've tortured myself with every memory of her from the moment we met, through the strained year that our love grew under her mother's watchful eye, throughout the year I had her all to myself, then finally the night before she ran from me.

The memory of that last night is as detailed as the rest. It's a memory worn thin from so much handling just like all the others. I've tormented myself with all of the ways I could've prevented her from leaving. If only I'd known her plan. If only I'd known her deception.

She kissed me as always that night. She slept in my arms, as always. She begged my forgiveness for angering me earlier in the day, as always. She took her punishment, as always. She was sweet and loving, as always.

I was perhaps a little angrier with her than I should have been. I was perhaps harsher than I usually was with her. Perhaps I applied the whip a little heavier than normal...

But it was for her own good. I told her that night that she was going to be my wife as soon as she finished school. She had to learn to control her mental states. Her outbursts and indulgences into child-like behavior had to stop. At the very least, she needed to become more adept at hiding them.

The specialists I'd hired said they had helped, that they'd given her ways to pull herself together. They all talked in circles about how her need to protect herself overpowered her need to merge her memories and shared experiences. All psycho-babble excuses for why I overpaid them and Gillian wasn't improved.

That last night, I made it clear that my patience with her behavior was over. I made it clear that I expected her to stay in control, to stay my sweet, loving Gillian. I made it clear what I would do if her other personalities showed themselves again.

I smile at my reflection in the window. The sky is already darkened from the fog that stole in quickly while I mused through my memories. I smile remembering Gillian's screams that night.

I'd forced her to stay present during her punishment. I forced her to not turn herself off like she was so capable of usually. I forced her to feel every lick of my whip, but I didn't let her enjoy it either. I wouldn't let her turn herself over to her masochistic desires, the personality that took all of her punishments before.

I made her stay my sweet, soft Gillian.

My whip and threats did what a team of doctors couldn't. I cured her that night. She stayed with me, not hiding inside herself or behind her unreadable stares. All her little cracks filled in with her desire to please me. She stayed in control and promised to be good. And I believed her.

She lied and deceived me, and she ran the next day.

I won't give her a chance to run and make a fool of me again.

Anderson Valley: Simon Lamb

Grace stands in front of my bedroom door. She's dressed but won't move out of the way. "You know that you're not really blocking the door, right?" I grin at her.

"I know you won't hurt me, Simon."

"Have you looked in a mirror today, sweetheart?" I try for threatening, but it falls short. I know she's right. Red I could hurt, and she'd like it. Grace and all her other versions…fuck. I can't hurt her at all. "Fine. I won't hurt you. *That's* why you need to go, Grace."

"It's why I need to stay, Simon."

I laugh, exasperated with this circular logic again. She's been trying to convince me to let her stay, and we've been back and forth getting nowhere. When I threatened to leave her here, locked in the room alone until she dressed, she finally did, but she kept her string of reasoning going the whole time.

"That doesn't make sense."

"Maybe not to you, but it does to us."

Fuck. There it is again. Us. It's insane how quickly I've gotten used to talking to her like she's a committee. "So why does it make sense to you?" I can feel that I'm losing ground. I don't really want to take her back to the city, but I think it's the right thing to do. I've never been big on right and wrong, only on getting what I want. Yet, I feel an overwhelming urge to protect her, even from myself. She hasn't said anything so far that's convinced me that I'm making a mistake.

"Because you accept me. Just as we are." I'm getting used to her crazy way too quickly. She's right though. I didn't even really blink an eye at finding out that she truly is batshit nuts. I accepted it as the only answer that ultimately explained all of the other craziness I knew about her.

It explained my crazy reaction to her too. I want to be soft and open for her just as much as I want to torture her. My response to her has splintered into equal parts of familiar and unfamiliar.

"So?"

"So. We accept you too. Just as you are." It's her first argument that packs a punch—a crazy punch.

"You accept that I get off on torture? That I was willing to kidnap you and keep you here against your will?"

"Yes." I expect her to say something more, but she only continues to blink at me.

"This is crazy, Grace!" I regret the word choice as soon I say it, but she only smiles sweeter at me and laughs a little. I can't help but laugh too.

"Let me ask you something, Simon…and answer me with complete honesty, okay?"

"I've been honest so far, so why stop now?"

She takes a deep breath. "Would you have threatened or hurt me when I was playing with my breakfast earlier, when I was a child that was too young to form many words even?" I shake my head, remembering her as she was this morning and at the diner. I was thinking she was a mess and completely adorable—not a word I'm comfortable using normally. I had that protective urge again too, not wanting her to notice the stares from the staff.

"How about when I'm shy and sheltered, like I was in Chinatown, scared of my own shadow?" I shake my head again. I saw Grace for the first time when she was like that. It's what drew me to her. But now, knowing what I know, I couldn't hurt her if she was like that again. I'd want to protect her, to give her as much space or as little or whatever the fuck else she'd need to make her feel safer.

"And if I'm wild with anger and fear?"

"Like with the poker yesterday?" She nods. "No. I wouldn't let you hurt yourself or anyone else either though." She smiles again, and my stomach sinks. My heart thumps too loudly in my ears. Fuck.

"And how about now?" Her sweet voice takes on a little of the huskiness—the bashful lust I saw from her this morning. She puts her hands on my chest, and her warmth is almost searing. I feel a lump in my throat that I can't swallow down. I can only shake my head. "But you want to hurt the girl you like to call Red, don't you?" I shake my head, but it's not convincing to either of us. I want to hurt the shit out of *that* girl.

She smiles. "The girl you whipped yesterday. The girl you…had sex with before…she likes pain. She doesn't feel it like the rest of us. She's like you…what frightens us, excites her."

I put my hands over hers. "But you'd all feel the pain of what I'd do to your body eventually." I move my hands to her shirt, gently gliding over her stiff nipples. Her gasp is a moan of pleasure though, not the painful wince I was expecting.

Her eyes close more. "We have great control of my body, Simon." It's an airy, eerie voice—one I've heard from her before. It's a strange mix of her soft sweetness and huskier depth, a fog circling around each word in a slightly halting tempo. When she opens her eyes again, her voice is back to normal, the normal sweet, soft tone anyway. "I don't like pain, but I can ignore it. I can pull myself in just enough to never feel what happens to me. I've done this all my life. We all have."

I can see the abused little girl she must have been, the one that had to become what she is now in order to survive. What monster hurt such a sweet girl? "I can't hurt you more than you've already been hurt, Grace. I'm an asshole, an abusive prick…but I can't. I said you wouldn't have choices with me, and you still don't. I'm taking you back."

"And I told you, Simon. You can't break me. We're already broken." She smiles, and I'm just about lost. "But you *can* accept me, and that's good enough for us. For now." She stretches up and puts her lips close to mine. "Is it good enough for you to be accepted?"

I should grab her and get the hell out of here. I should drag her ass back to San Francisco and out of my life. I should, but I don't.

I'm a bad, bad man.

Instead, I grab her and lift her straight up, holding her against me, pressing our lips together in a hard kiss, a kiss that says what I can't. It's a kiss that says what I won't admit—I want her, I need her. All of her batshit craziness, it's what I crave.

Her arms wrap around me, and I carry her back to my bed. Her lips stay soft against mine; her tongue seeks me out but gently—our sweet dance. I set her down, but her hands keep pulling me to her.

I pry her arms loose and give her a wicked grin. If this is going to work, then she needs to get used to playing by my rules. She frowns and smiles; her shy looks make me harder.

"Get undressed, Grace." She seems nervous. Her fingers fidget and fly over her clothes, trying to get them off quickly for me. I don't help her, just keep watching. Grace has a matching red bra and underwear set on. It's sweet but still sexy. "Stop right there."

The marks on her body are graffiti on her creamy canvas. Most are fading, but some are thicker and heavier in places. I run my hands gently over her shoulders and down her sides. She shivers and wiggles for me.

I lean over and whisper in her ear, "Stay still, sweet girl." She smiles her answer.

I run my hands back up her stomach, over her tits and chest, feeling the deeper welts. Amazingly, Grace gasps in need, her hunger obvious, her eyes closing partially. I know she said she could withdraw herself from the pain, but I'm still in awe of her. I'm being gentle, but I know it has to sting in spots.

"Now you can finish undressing for me." She opens her eyes, and the sweetness I see there is only made deeper by the lust that has her cheeks flushed. She quickly removes everything and stands ready for me. She may be innocent, but she's also very submissive, giving in to her pleasure at pleasing me with her obedience.

I pull her face to mine, rubbing my thumbs over her cheeks. I still wince seeing the bruise next to her beautiful mouth. Her smile changes and a laugh enters her voice. "Would it help if I hit *you*, Simon?" I bring my eyes back up to hers and can see more laughter waiting to spill.

"You better never, sweetheart." But I smile at her too. I whisper a kiss over the side of her mouth. I have no idea how any of this will work out, but right now, I don't give a shit. I just want her, and she's right; I want all of her, even if that means only getting a piece at a time.

I stand back and get my own clothes off quickly. Grace is still nervous, still tentative, but her eyes aren't bashful anymore. She follows my every move, licking her lips even. I put my thumb against her lower lip, ignoring the bruise now, just as Grace is so easily able to do. She opens and sucks my thumb, her eyes pleading for more—pleading her desire to please me.

"On the bed." She makes me laugh by falling backwards, arms out like a child in the snow. She reaches with her hands out to me. I collapse on top of her, feeling a strange longing to stay in her embrace. I want to lose whole days feeling her warmth, claiming every inch of her, stealing all her sweet smiles with a kiss.

Her hips moving under me take my thoughts in a different direction though. I push her legs open with mine. Her hips tilt, and she brings her legs up around my waist. Our lips find each other just as I enter her. Her soft cry out fills my mouth.

I'm not as gentle this time. I push into her with more need, and she responds with her own. We stay close, pressing every inch together that we can. Our lips never leave each other. I lift her off the bed with one hand under her, pushing her to me, me to her. Our hips move together, only apart as far as we can reach without letting go, then smashing together as tight as possible. Our grunts are in sync. Panting heavily, we come together. I don't let her go, staying in her as long as I can, smothering her body and mouth.

When our skin grows cold, I finally move to her side. She whimpers when our lips are no longer touching. I prop myself up on my elbow so I can look down on her, tracing the lines of her face with one finger. "You are such a sweet girl, Grace. I'll never hurt you. I promise." She kisses my finger when I brush over her lips, over her smile. I look up and see the syrup sitting on the nightstand. "Oh, damn. I meant to use that on you."

She laughs her deep laugh. I know before looking down that she's changed; she's no longer the soft, sweet version I just made love to. Her mischievous grin is back. "Save the sweet stuff, Trust. *I* prefer what's in your cabinet."

I lean down and kiss her throat; she laughs for me again. "Stay right here, Red." I move off the bed. When I reach the armoire, I turn around to look at her.

She stretches out for me, opening her legs and putting her hands over her head. She's a perfect invitation to use and abuse her—a wanton lust for what she knows comes next. I have no idea how any of this can work, but I think I just hit the jackpot. I can have my sweet cake and beat it too.

Anderson Valley: Simon Lamb

"You're beautiful, sweetheart." I kiss Red's hand, walking with her down the curved stairs. She's in a long red dress. It's not as flashy as the one I first saw her in, but it's just as form fitting, showing off all of her body. The low neckline doesn't leave any doubt that she still prefers to go without undergarments, but the high back hides the marks from my favorite whip. She knows I prefer those to be for my eyes only.

"My cousin will want to fuck you." She smiles wickedly at that. I slap her ass hard, and she laughs her deep throat filling laugh she knows I love. I kiss her neck before she stops, growling against her, "Behave, or I'll have Grace take your place tonight."

She pouts, pushing her red lip out as an invitation to bite. When I don't take the bait, she shrugs, moving away from me and over to the drinks set on a table. "You promised. You said I would be better company around your cousin."

"I *said* you'd have more fun with Cary than Grace would." She turns to face me again and smiles like I just agreed with her. "But that doesn't mean I'll let you fuck him. Or any other man, Red." This reminds me. "One last thing. For tonight…your name is Scarlet." She raises her eyebrows for a second, then shrugs once more.

This also reminds me to try to get her real name out of her again. The frustration is starting to wear on me, but I return her smile, just watching her move. I've spent every minute of every day around her for four weeks now, and Grace has only given me a few details about herself, nothing from before her arrival in San Francisco. Red has been even more tight-lipped.

Watching the sway of her hips under the dress, I can't blame myself for being distracted though. Sex has been insane. Ha, that's an understatement. It's almost like a threesome at times, switching between what Grace likes and what Red craves, with only the barest pause between the two. All of my own needs have been met, more than I ever thought possible.

I've joked that they almost seem to fight over me in bed. That joke didn't go over well with either of them. I rub my chin absentmindedly, still feeling where Red's head hit me when she tried to indignantly jump out of bed a few days ago. She laughed and said I deserved worse for bringing up Grace while with her. I laughed too since it had been Grace in my bed only a second before.

And I'm still shocked at how calmly I've accepted all of this. I've gotten so used to the switching back and forth that I don't even notice it. I'm able to anticipate her changes, and she's able to anticipate my needs.

Her past is still a mystery to me, but *she* no longer is. None of her five versions are.

Grace is all soft and yielding. I hold my breath more when I'm with her, like the slightest shift in atmosphere could cause her pain. No. Not pain, she doesn't feel any. More like she's so sensitive to everything and everyone around her that I want to bubble wrap her against the world. I feel more protective of her than I do even for the version that draws all over my breakfast table each morning.

I chuckle thinking about the raised brows from my staff when I only laughed at the first artistic alterations to my furniture. That table has been in my family for longer than I've been alive. I don't give a shit. My first thought when I looked down at the scribbles and scrawl marks on the inlaid surface was how like a winemaker my Little Grace is. She took something hard and unmoving and brought it to life— remade it into something to be used and enjoyed, not just admired or preserved.

She's done that with everything, twisted it all around so I can't remember what it was like to not have her here.

The version of her I think of as Miss Smartypants Grace has made herself at home in my office, surrounded by books and computer programs. She makes me wait in the dining room each night for her to come down with her daily predictions for me. Most of it is a rundown of the day's events, but every once in a while, she throws in a prediction for some future date. She said last night's was about today. It had something to do with unfamiliar waters and important choices. *There's* another understatement.

The doorbell rings, and I walk into my foyer to meet Cary just as the door is opened. I was surprised when I got his call yesterday. I've not avoided him, but I've turned down all of his requests to visit me in San Francisco lately. I haven't mentioned Grace either.

When he said that he wanted to come here, I couldn't think of a reason to say no; I could think of five reasons. I laugh to myself, but I may as well get it over with. I have no idea how long this thing with Grace will last, but I know that I want her to meet my family.

And that's batshit crazy coming from me. Talk about unfamiliar waters.

We hug and I pull Cary towards the grand hall quickly. "I want you to meet someone." He raises his brows. I stop him with a hand to his chest. "No. Not like that. She's not a product." He raises his brows even higher, but I ignore this.

We walk past a table with a big vase of fresh cut roses. I smirk at these, just another example of Grace exasperating my staff of late. This time it was the version I think of as

Hellcat Grace. I found her out in the garden yesterday, chopping at the roses in a fit. I just stood and watched as she grunted and went at the petal heads like they were royal lineage in Robespierre's France. She exhausted herself quickly, the clippers tossed with a loud clang to the bricked pathway.

Still, I just watched to see what she would do next. Try to clean up and hide what she'd done? Kick the petals around? Start speaking in tongues and spew green soup? I didn't know, but it came as no shock to me by then that I *wanted* to know. I've come to terms with the fact that I'm obsessed with knowing every part of her.

Hellcat just turned to me like she knew I was there the whole time. She sort of grinned at me. At least, I think she did. She was gone too quickly for me to be sure. Grace replaced her, and the tears she started to shed for all the lost flowers was enough to have me pulling her into my arms before my feet even stopped moving toward her. I shushed and held her until Grace finally believed that I didn't care about silly flowers. I only cared about her.

I didn't let Grace pick up the severed blooms; her hands would've been a bloody mess from all the thorns. Instead, I let her arrange them in the vase when the gardening staff brought them in. She smelled like roses when we went to bed.

I'm brought out of my thoughts by Cary whistling when we enter my main sitting room. Red turns around to smile at him. "You must be Cary, the sweet cousin that Simon thinks will try to charm the panties off me." Cary laughs. I don't. I give her a warning look, but she ignores me, walking forward to shake hands with him.

"I'll certainly do my best."

Red leans into him a little more. "Good thing for you, I don't wear any." They laugh together like old friends. I can see my cousin eye fucking her, looking her up and down and not letting go of her hand.

The irrational kind of anger that I don't normally feel chokes me. Hell, I never feel this way except around her. I have a desire to order her back upstairs, to lock her in my room. Fuck that. Lock her in the cave.

But I haven't shown her that yet. I haven't wanted to scare her, not that anything scares Red. It might scare Grace, though, or the others.

This thought calms me a little. I clear my throat, and Cary finally lets her hand go. She walks over to the drinks and grabs one for each of us. She brings mine over to me with her most wicked grin. I give her another warning look. She puts her arm in mine and smiles more sweetly, not Grace's sweet smile but a sarcastic version of it.

I lean over to whisper in her ear. "Behave yourself, Red. I've not had to give you a punishment whipping yet, but you're well on your way to earning one tonight."

She smiles brighter. "Promises, promises."

"So, how did you two meet?" Cary interrupts us, stepping closer and giving me a strange look. I know I won't hear the end of his questions until he has every detail. Well, every detail that I'm willing to give him anyway.

I'm saved by the bell this time though. My doorbell chime has Cary putting down his drink and moving towards the foyer again. I frown at him. "Expecting someone?"

Cary sheepishly smiles at me. "Yes, I'll explain in a second, cuz." He disappears towards the foyer. Red shrugs and heads to the drink she left on the table. I turn to the door just as Cary walks in with a tall, dark haired man. He's about my age, thin but muscular, expensively dressed.

Cary starts talking fast, introducing the guy before they've even reached me. "I didn't get a chance to tell my cousin about your interest in a particular product he might be able to obtain for you." Cary nods to me, doing a poor job of trying to act like he's not talking in code while he obviously is. "I'm sure you can better describe your needs anyway."

The man smiles at me, but I can see that his eyes are on Red behind me, obviously looking her up and down. That pit of anger is back, and I shoot a glare at Cary. He pushes himself in closer to us. "Simon, meet Miles Vanderson."

The story concludes with

we were one once book 2

WILLOW MADISON

we were one once
book 2

Madison